Misfit

A Tale of Secrets, Loyalties, and Unlikely Bonds

Author
Rebeccah Worship

Rebeccah Worship

Gratitude

With heartfelt gratitude, I extend my deepest thanks to the incredible people, organizations, and communities that have guided and supported me throughout my writing journey.

To the *Salvation Army* and *Our Daily Bread*, your unwavering commitment to uplifting lives inspired me to find strength in every circumstance. Your compassion and service embody the values I hope to reflect in my stories.

To *Galveston Central Church* and *Grace Clinic*, thank you for being beacons of hope and encouragement. Your kindness and support created a foundation of faith and resilience that helped me persevere through challenges.

To *Galveston Housing Plus* and *Rosenberg Library*, your resources, guidance, and spaces of learning have been invaluable. You nurtured my creativity and provided me with the tools to bring this story to life.

And to the *City of Galveston*, thank you for being a vibrant backdrop to my journey, where inspiration flows as freely as the waves on your shores.

This novella would not exist without the collective impact of each of you. I am forever grateful for the role you've played in shaping both this story and the writer I've become.

With all my love and appreciation, Rebeccah Worship

Misfit

Rebeccah Worship

Copyright Disclaimer

Rebeccah Worship

Misfit

TABLE OF CONTENTS

Rebeccah Worship

"*How many times must I tell you, Priscilla, my love life—or lack of it—is not a group project?*" Temilola Adeniyi said, leveling a sharp stare at her daughter across the gleaming marble counter. Yet Priscilla's mischievous grin suggested she'd already made her move.

Temilola Adeniyi's life was a masterstroke of meticulous design, where every note of her existence hummed with intention. Her days unfolded like a symphony, each moment orchestrated to perfection, every detail aligned to a greater rhythm she had composed. And nowhere was this harmony clearer than in her sprawling penthouse, perched high above the frenetic pace of Lagos. It was a sanctuary, a breathtaking blend of boldness and refinement, much like the woman herself.

The living room was a vibrant homage to her roots, adorned with intricately woven Aso Oke pillows that splashed their colors—sunset orange, deep indigo, and emerald green—

against the minimalist canvas of her modular white sofa. Hand-carved wooden sculptures, sourced from a hidden artisan's studio in Ibadan, stood like sentinels along a wall of glass that framed the sprawling city below. A sleek chrome-and-glass coffee table anchored the room, atop which lay art books and a single vase holding a protea bloom, as if to declare her love for beauty in all its forms. The space spoke to Temilola's duality: a woman who could appreciate the raw elegance of tradition while thriving in the crisp clarity of the modern world.

Yet, for all its grandeur, the penthouse was more than just a reflection of Temilola's taste—it was a shield. The curated aesthetic, with its calculated warmth and sophistication, spoke louder than any words. It told visitors, colleagues, and even casual acquaintances that this was a woman who had risen above. Above what, exactly, was a mystery Temilola guarded with fierce determination.

Her professional life was just as calculated. As the lead brand marketer at one of Lagos' top advertising agencies, she wielded words and imagery with the precision of a surgeon. Boardrooms buzzed with anticipation whenever she took the floor, her presentations a magnetic mix of compelling narratives and unassailable strategy. Temilola had the uncanny ability to take a nascent idea—a fragment of inspiration whispered in a brainstorming session—and transform it into a campaign that roared. Brands under her care didn't just thrive; they dominated, their stories etched into the collective consciousness of a city that never stopped moving.

Her success was undeniable, her ambition enviable. Colleagues marveled at her ability to navigate the high-pressure world of advertising, where deadlines loomed like dark clouds, and competition was as cutthroat as the Lagos traffic below her penthouse. She seemed to thrive on the chaos, finding order in the madness and bending it to her will. It was perhaps her greatest strength—this ability to project calm while masterminding storms of creativity.

But for all her accomplishments, there was an emptiness, a quiet ache she refused to acknowledge. It hovered at the edges of her days, a formless void she drowned in client briefs and late-night strategy sessions. She wore power suits like armor, their clean lines and bold hues a defiant declaration that she was in control. And yet, in the solitude of her penthouse, with the city lights twinkling like distant stars, Temilola often felt a hollowness she couldn't quite place.

Her life, for all its precision, was incomplete. It was as though she had painted a masterpiece and left a single corner of the canvas blank, afraid to fill it in for fear of what the final picture might reveal. The past, with its shadows and scars, lingered just beyond the reach of her carefully curated world. It was a chapter she refused to read, much less write, and so she busied herself with the present—

polished, powerful, and seemingly perfect.

Rebeccah Worship

Chapter 1: The Price of Perfection

In the stillness of her home, amid the interplay of textures and tones she had so lovingly selected, Temilola Adeniyi often found herself wondering: *Was this enough? Could a life so vividly designed ever truly silence the whisper of what was missing?* She pushed the thought away as she always did, reaching instead for the next campaign, the next challenge, the next proof that she could thrive in the face of anything. Because Temilola Adeniyi was nothing if not resilient, even when the symphony of her life played a note of longing that only she could hear.

The heartbeat of Temilola's world, the force that often unraveled her otherwise perfectly controlled life, was her daughter, Priscilla. At 22, Priscilla was the embodiment of youthful fire—a tempest of ideas and dreams wrapped in an easy, infectious smile. Her energy was magnetic, her laughter an echo of the girl Temilola had once been. Priscilla was the living testament to everything Temilola had sacrificed: every late night, every struggle, every choice that placed stability and success above personal desire.

Priscilla, however, was not one to stay confined to her mother's well-ordered narrative. She was a whirlwind of independence and ambition, studying architecture at the University of Lagos while juggling an entrepreneurial streak that made Temilola proud—and exhausted. Priscilla's ideas were as big as her personality: sustainable urban spaces for underserved communities, eco-friendly building materials, and grand designs that seamlessly blended tradition with innovation. Temilola marveled at how her daughter's dreams mirrored her own values in such a distinct and fearless way.

But lately, Priscilla had taken up a new project—her mother. It started innocently enough: gentle teasing about the absence of male voices in the house, playful remarks during quiet dinners about the silence of Temilola's phone when it wasn't ringing for work.

"Mummy, you know WhatsApp has these status updates where people share their 'soft life' moments. Yours is just work, work, work. Do you even know how to have fun anymore?" Priscilla would say, her eyes sparkling with a mischief Temilola had no defense against.

Temilola had laughed it off at first, brushing away her daughter's comments with a dismissive wave or a pointed change of subject. But Priscilla wasn't one to let things go. She had inherited her mother's tenacity, after all, and this new mission was no different.

"You're in voluntary romantic exile," Priscilla declared one evening, as they shared bowls of steaming jollof rice in the penthouse dining room. "I'm just saying, it's not healthy. You're hiding in this workaholic bubble when the world outside is full of possibilities."

"Possibilities?" Temilola raised a brow, reaching for her glass of water. "I've had my fill of 'possibilities.' They're overrated."

"No, Mum. What's overrated is pretending you're fine when you're not," Priscilla shot back, her tone a careful balance of love and exasperation. "You deserve happiness. The kind you don't schedule into your Google Calendar."

The words hit harder than Temilola cared to admit. She was a woman who thrived on structure, who had rebuilt her life brick by careful brick, ensuring there were no cracks for disappointment to seep through. Romance, with all its unpredictability and vulnerability, was a crack she couldn't risk reopening. Not after Priscilla's father had walked out when she was barely a toddler, leaving Temilola to shoulder the weight of their future alone. She had vowed then that love would never be a distraction again.

But Priscilla saw through the facade. Her persistence came with warmth, a refusal to let her mother remain cocooned in her fortress of solitude. One day, she emailed Temilola a link to a "speed dating for professionals" event with a note that read, *"Mummy, you market brands for a living; now market yourself…don't worry, I'll oversee the dress. You can cancel if you want, but if you go, I promise to stop teasing you for a whole month."*

"Priscilla, you didn't," Temilola groaned when she saw the email.

The deal was tempting. Not because Temilola had any intention of showing up at the event, but because she recognized her daughter's efforts for what they were: an act of love. Beneath Priscilla's playful jabs and relentless meddling lay a profound desire to see her mother live fully, not just exist in the polished shell of success she had created.

That night, after Priscilla had retreated to her room with her textbooks and sketch pads, Temilola sat by the floor-to-ceiling windows of her penthouse, watching the city's lights flicker like stars. Her daughter's words lingered, a soft whisper in the back of her mind. *You deserve happiness.*

Did she? And if so, where would she even begin to find it? The idea scared her more than she was ready to admit.

Chapter 2: Networking for Feelings

Temilola sighed deeply, glancing at her daughter sprawled on the plush sectional sofa, phone in hand, face alight with a determination that was both endearing and exasperating. "Priscilla," she began, her tone deliberate, "I'm not a teenager. And I certainly don't need you playing matchmaker with strangers on the internet."

Priscilla barely looked up, her thumb still scrolling. "It's not matchmaking, Mum. It's modern networking... but for feelings." Her eyes flicked back to the screen. "Oh, wait! This guy has a yacht! Look at his profile pic—he's got main character energy."

Temilola pinched the bridge of her nose, leaning back in her chair. "I don't need a man with a yacht, Priscilla. Or any man, for that matter. I'm perfectly fine as I am."

Priscilla rolled her eyes in that theatrical way only a 22-year-old could. "You keep saying that, but you don't mean it. You're fine, yes. But you're not happy. You're like… comfortably numb." She sat up suddenly, setting the phone aside. Her face softened. "Mum, you've spent your whole life making sure I had everything I needed. And you've crushed it. Look at me—independent, thriving, and clearly the superior Adeniyi." She smirked, waiting for the obligatory eye roll from her mother, which came on cue. Then her tone turned serious. "But who's looking out for you? Don't you deserve someone who makes you feel seen?"

Temilola stared at her daughter, caught off guard by the sincerity behind the words. It wasn't the first time Priscilla had ventured into these waters, but tonight her plea felt different—deeper, more purposeful.

"You think I don't feel seen?" Temilola asked quietly, folding her arms across her chest. It was a defensive gesture, one Priscilla didn't miss.

Priscilla hesitated, as if weighing her response. "I think you're so good at making sure people see the version of you that you've perfected—the powerhouse, the brand genius, the boss lady in heels—that you've forgotten what it's like to let someone see the messy, vulnerable you. The real you."

The words hit a nerve. Temilola looked away, her gaze landing on the protea bloom in its vase. She had chosen it for its resilience, its ability to thrive in harsh conditions. It was a flower that didn't wilt easily—a metaphor she had always found comforting. But now, under her daughter's perceptive gaze, the flower seemed to mock her.

"Priscilla," she began, her voice softening, "it's not that simple. Letting someone in means risking everything. Again. And I've already done that. It didn't end well."

"You're talking about Dad," Priscilla said, her tone gentle but firm. She leaned forward, resting her elbows on her knees. "But Mum, you've been carrying that fear for twenty years. You've rebuilt this incredible life, one that inspires me every single day. Don't let him keep you stuck in that old hurt. He doesn't get to define what comes next for you."

Temilola's breath hitched. It wasn't like her daughter to talk about her father; Priscilla had long accepted his absence with a grace that astonished Temilola. Yet, here she was, dredging up the past in an effort to guide her mother into the future.

"I'm not stuck," Temilola said after a long pause, though her voice lacked conviction.

Priscilla smiled faintly, shaking her head. "You're stuck, Mum. But it's okay. We all get stuck sometimes. That's why you have me—to push you forward."

Temilola wanted to argue, to insist she was content, fulfilled, even happy in her own way. But the truth lingered between them like an unspoken secret. Priscilla had seen through the facade Temilola worked so hard to maintain, and it both terrified and comforted her.

"Alright," Temilola said finally, with a sigh that felt as heavy as the years she had spent avoiding this conversation. "You get one shot, Priscilla. But if this 'networking for feelings' nonsense backfires, you're washing the dishes for a month."

Priscilla's squeal of delight filled the penthouse. "Deal!" she exclaimed, already reaching for her phone again. "Now, let's talk about what you're wearing for your first date…"

Temilola buried her face in her hands, laughing despite herself. Perhaps this would end in disaster. Or perhaps, for the first time in years, it was a risk worth taking.

Chapter 3: The Hall of Dating Horrors

What followed was a whirlwind of blind dates—each more bizarre than the last, as though Priscilla had curated them for maximum chaos rather than compatibility.

The first was an ethical hacker named Bayo, who looked promising enough on paper. He was tall, with an easy smile and a sharp wit that Temilola found refreshing—for about ten minutes. Then, over a plate of grilled tilapia at a trendy Victoria Island restaurant, Bayo launched into a soliloquy about the futility of modern relationships.

"I mean, everything is just algorithms, right?" he said, gesturing with his fork like a philosopher addressing his acolytes. "Even love. Swipe left, swipe right, like it's all pre-programmed. Are we even choosing anything, or are we just... puppets?"

Temilola blinked, her carefully applied eyeliner concealing the twitch of irritation. "I'm fairly certain I chose this tilapia," she said dryly, but Bayo was too deep in his existential spiral to notice.

By the time the waiter brought their dessert, Temilola was already counting the minutes until she could escape. Bayo, undeterred by her growing silence, continued his monologue with the fervor of someone discovering existentialism for the first time. "And think about it," he pressed on, his fork now pointing toward her as if she were a co-conspirator in his revelations. "If love is just chemistry and timing, what's the point of all this... effort?"

Temilola forced a polite smile, taking a sip of her drink. "The effort," she said with deliberate calm, "is what separates humans from, say, goldfish. You know, the ability to care, connect, and, occasionally, listen."

For the first time, Bayo paused, his brow furrowing as though she'd just asked him to explain quantum mechanics. But the moment was fleeting. "Oh, I do listen," he assured her, leaning back in his chair with the confidence of a man who had not heard a word. "In fact, listening is part of hacking. You listen to systems, to patterns, to—"

Temilola's phone buzzed on the table, cutting him off mid-lecture. She glanced down at the screen to see a message from Priscilla:

How's it going? Do we love him, hate him, or tolerate him?

With Bayo still gesturing animatedly about algorithms and puppets, Temilola typed back: *Tilapia is great. Man is a TED Talk in disguise. Pray for me.*

When the check finally arrived, Temilola resisted the urge to leap from her seat in triumph. As they stepped outside, the warm Lagos night wrapping around them, Bayo turned to her with a self-satisfied grin. "This was fun," he said. "We should do it again sometime. Maybe next time, I'll tell you about my theories on digital immortality."

Temilola's smile was tight, her nod even tighter. "I'll... think about it," she replied, mentally making a note to block his number the moment she got into her car.

Next came Kunle, the professional mourner. He arrived at the café down the street from her penthouse dressed head-to-toe in black, his face set in an expression so somber it felt like the funeral he'd just left was his own. At first, Temilola thought it was a quirky sense of humor, but when Kunle began tearing up while describing a particularly moving dirge he'd performed, she realized this wasn't a bit.

"Emotions are my currency," he said, his voice trembling as he clutched his coffee cup like it contained the ashes of a lost love. "To grieve is to live, you know?"

"I think I've grieved enough for one lifetime," Temilola muttered under her breath, wondering how she would explain this one to Priscilla.

By the time Kunle began reciting his poetry—his own original composition, naturally—Temilola was certain the evening was destined for the Hall of Dating Horrors.

"The heart," he began, his voice low and dramatic, "is a fragile vessel. A bird caged, yearning to sing but shackled by the weight of—"

"Kunle," Temilola interrupted, raising a hand to stop the deluge of metaphors. "This is... fascinating. Truly. But do you ever talk about, you know, lighter things? Hobbies? Travel? The weather, even?"

Kunle blinked, as though the concept of lightheartedness was utterly alien to him. "Ah," he said after a pause, his expression grave, "but to focus on trivialities is to deny the depths of the human experience. Don't you think?"

"No," she replied flatly, taking a long sip of her cappuccino. "I think sometimes you just need to laugh at a good meme."

Kunle tilted his head, studying her with the same intensity one might reserve for a work of abstract art. "Interesting," he murmured. "You have the air of someone who's endured much. Perhaps that's why you shy away from the abyss."

Temilola set her cup down with a soft clink, summoning every ounce of restraint to keep her composure. "Kunle," she said, "it's not the abyss I'm avoiding. It's the performance of it."

As she walked away from Kunle's dramatic parting words, the cool night air wrapped around her like an embrace. Her phone buzzed again:

If you ever set me up with another tortured poet, I'm disowning you.

LOL! What happened? Details! Priscilla replied.

Temilola shook her head, her lips curving into a reluctant smile. *Let's just say I learned more about dirges than I ever wanted to.*

Whahala. Okay, no more artistes. Let's try a tech brah next?

Laughing softly, Temilola slipped her phone into her bag. She wasn't sure if she could survive a tech bro, but at this point, anything seemed better than reliving Kunle's endless dirges. At least she was stepping outside the confines of her curated world.

For now, that was enough.

Rebeccah Worship

Chapter 4: Stains and Stories

Fatai, the crime scene cleaner, greeted Temilola with a firm handshake that quickly escalated into an uncomfortably relentless squeeze, leaving her instinctively pulling back. Over dinner at an upscale bar and grill in Ikoyi, surrounded by romantic candlelight and soft music, Fatai's enthusiasm for his line of work became abundantly clear—and increasingly unsettling.

"You wouldn't believe the kinds of stains people leave behind," he began, leaning in closer than necessary. "But I don't just clean— I restore. It's an art, really."

Temilola offered a polite nod, subtly inching her chair back as the word *handsy* flashed in her mind like a neon warning sign.

Fatai continued undeterred, his animated gestures punctuating every word as he described the intricacies of his craft with almost theatrical fervor. "The trick to blood," he whispered conspiratorially, "is hydrogen peroxide. But brain matter? Now *that* requires finesse."

Temilola froze mid-bite, her fork hovering inches from her mouth. "Brain matter?" she echoed, her voice tinged with incredulity.

"Hypothetically speaking," he clarified with a grin that did little to ease her growing discomfort. "You know, the toughest stains always tell the best stories."

Swallowing her rising unease, Temilola reached for her water glass, hoping the cool liquid would steady her nerves. "That's... quite a unique perspective," she said, carefully avoiding any tone that might encourage further elaboration.

Fatai beamed, his expression radiating pride—or perhaps self-absorption. "It's all in the details," he continued, lowering his voice as if revealing a profound truth. "Details separate the amateurs from the professionals. Did you know you can tell a person's emotional state from the way they—"

The sharp buzz of Temilola's phone vibrating on the table was her saving grace. "Excuse me," she said, snatching the device with barely concealed urgency. The screen lit up with Priscilla's name, and Temilola silently thanked her daughter's impeccable timing.

She stood, offering a quick apology before stepping away to answer. "Priscilla, you have no idea how perfectly you just saved me," she whispered, her voice tinged with both relief and exasperation.

Her daughter's reply was laced with amusement. "That bad, huh?"

Temilola cast a cautious glance back at the table, where Fatai was now meticulously arranging the napkins like a crime scene reconstruction. "Let's just say he'd fit in better at a true crime convention than on a date."

Priscilla's laughter was so loud Temilola had to hold the phone away from her ear. "Mum, you should start a podcast. *Dating Disasters with Temilola.*"

"Very funny," Temilola muttered, though she couldn't suppress a small smile. "Now, how do I end this gracefully?"

"Tell him you've been summoned to a board meeting," Priscilla suggested with mock seriousness. "Or that you're allergic to crime scene stories. Either works."

Rolling her eyes, Temilola ended the call and took a steadying breath before returning to the table.

"Everything alright?" Fatai asked, his intense gaze as unwavering as his handshake.

"Unfortunately, I have to cut this short," Temilola said, summoning her most professional tone. "Work emergency. You know how it is."

Fatai's face fell briefly before he rallied. "Of course," he said, rising to his feet and reaching for her hand. "It's been a pleasure, Temilola. Truly."

Bracing herself for another crushing handshake, she was relieved when he showed some restraint this time. As she walked away, she could feel his gaze lingering, undimmed by her abrupt departure.

Once in her car, she exhaled a long sigh, her carefully maintained composure cracking as she leaned back against the seat. Her phone buzzed with a message from Priscilla: *So, when's the wedding?*

She chuckled, typing back: *I'll let you know when I stop running for my life.*

Priscilla's response came almost immediately, a string of laughing emojis followed by: *Okay, no more crime scene cleaners.*

How about a pilot? Or a chef? Or both! Imagine the meals AND the private jets!

Shaking her head, Temilola tucked her phone away. As exhausting as these dates were, they served as a reminder that even the most meticulously curated life couldn't shield her from the chaos of the unexpected. And maybe, just maybe, that wasn't entirely a bad thing.

For now, though, she was content to retreat to her penthouse, pour herself a glass of wine, and laugh at the absurdity of it all. If love truly was an art, as Fatai had suggested, then perhaps her masterpiece was still a work in progress.

Chapter 5: The Treadmill of Change

After a night of excessive drinking in her luxurious penthouse, reflecting on her bizarre date with Fatai, Temilola awoke early the next morning with a renewed determination to hit the gym. She was eager to burn off the indulgences of the previous evening and maintain her enviable hourglass figure. But as fate would have it, this gym session would prove far more eventful than she anticipated.

It was there that she encountered Jasper— a young man she had seen countless times at networking events but had never spoken to. They moved in overlapping professional circles, sharing connections with the same business partners. Jasper, in his late 20s, had admired Temilola, who was in her mid-40s, from a distance for quite some time. Yet, Temilola's internalized fears about appearances and propriety had always kept her from acknowledging him.

Today, however, Jasper finally mustered the courage to bridge the gap. Spotting Temilola on a treadmill, he approached with two chilled bottles of water in hand and casually placed one on the treadmill beside hers before starting his jog.

As the pace of her treadmill increased, Temilola began to gasp for air, clearly pushing herself beyond her limits. Noticing her struggle, Jasper slowed his pace, picked up one of the water bottles, and offered it to her with an easy smile. "Electrolytes to replenish?"

Caught off guard by the gesture, Temilola reduced her treadmill speed to a walk and accepted the bottle with a murmured, "Thank you."

"You're welcome," Jasper replied, his grin warm and disarming. "Looked like you needed a quick break."

Temilola took a long sip of the cold water, letting its coolness soothe her parched throat. She glanced at Jasper from the corner of her eye, noting the effortless confidence in his posture and the calm steadiness of his gaze. Though younger, there was a maturity in his demeanor that intrigued her. His neatly trimmed beard framed his smile, which radiated a sincerity that felt rare.

"You're here early," Jasper remarked casually, keeping pace on his treadmill. "Most people wait until later in the day to avoid the crowd."

"I prefer the quiet," Temilola replied, still catching her breath. "Early mornings help me stay disciplined."

Jasper nodded thoughtfully. "That makes sense. Something about starting the day with a challenge sets the tone for the hours ahead."

Temilola raised an eyebrow. "Philosopher and fitness enthusiast?"

"More like a practical opportunist," he replied with a grin. "It's easier to focus when I'm not fighting over equipment with half of Lagos."

She chuckled despite herself, her tension easing ever so slightly. Still, a voice in her head cautioned her, whispering reminders about appearances and the unspoken rules she lived by. *He's too young, Temilola. What would they say?*

Jasper seemed unaware of her internal conflict. Slowing his treadmill to match her pace, he glanced at her with a thoughtful expression. "You know, I've seen you at a few events," he began. "You always seem so composed. But here, you're... different."

Temilola stiffened. "Different how?"

"More real," Jasper said without hesitation. "Less polished, more... approachable."

She wasn't sure if she should feel flattered or offended. *Polished* was her armor, the carefully cultivated image that shielded her from the judgmental world she inhabited. *Approachable* felt like a crack in that armor—an exposure she wasn't sure she wanted.

"Maybe the gym just makes everyone seem more human," she said lightly, deflecting his observation.

Jasper chuckled, unbothered by her guarded response. "Maybe. Or maybe it's the treadmill's magic—breaking down walls one mile at a time."

Temilola shook her head, but she couldn't suppress a smile. Jasper had a lightness about him, a refreshing ease that stood in stark contrast to the brooding intensity of the men she usually encountered.

"I'm Jasper, by the way," he said, extending a hand as they stepped off their treadmills.

"Temilola," she replied, shaking his hand briefly. His grip was firm yet gentle, his palm warm against hers.

"I know," he said with a teasing smile. "It's hard not to recognize Lagos' most formidable brand marketer."

She tilted her head, skeptical. "Formidable?"

"Absolutely," Jasper said earnestly. "Your campaigns are legendary. You take ideas and turn them into movements. It's impressive."

Temilola felt a flicker of pride but kept her expression neutral. "You seem to know a lot about me," she said. "What do you do, Jasper?"

"Business development," he replied. "I've worked with a few of your agency's clients. We've just never had the chance to talk."

"Well, we're talking now," she said, her tone carefully measured.

Jasper's smile softened. "We are. And I'm glad. You're not as intimidating as I thought you'd be."

The comment took her by surprise. "I'll take that as a compliment," she said cautiously.

"It is," he assured her. "And maybe, if you're up for it, we could grab a coffee sometime. You know, off the treadmill."

Temilola hesitated, her sensible side urging her to decline. But there was something about Jasper's straightforwardness that disarmed her. Against her better judgment, she nodded. "Maybe."

Jasper's grin widened. With a casual wave, he headed toward the weights area. Temilola watched him go, feeling a curious mix of intrigue and unease.

What would Priscilla think? the voice in her head whispered. She sighed, tightening the cap on her water bottle. Perhaps it was time to stop worrying about what others thought and start considering what *she* wanted.

Back at her penthouse, she crossed paths with her daughter, Priscilla, in the kitchen.

"Hi, Mummy. How was your workout?" Priscilla asked, her tone casual as she rummaged through the fridge.

"Uneventful," Temilola replied quickly, brushing past her with a touch of urgency. She hurried to her room, silently praying that the name *Jasper* wasn't written all over her face.

Chapter 6: Matchmaking Misdirection

After freshening up from her workout, Temilola entered the kitchen, where Priscilla sat perched at the island table. One hand held a snack, while the other scrolled through her phone.

"Mom," Priscilla began, her tone carefully casual, "I've decided I want a classy party at home for my 23rd birthday." She emphasized *classy* as if it would sweeten the pill of her request.

Temilola, still alert from her morning workout, gave her daughter a pointed look.

"Fine," she said after a pause, "but I'll oversee the decorations, food, and drinks."

Priscilla groaned, throwing her hands in the air dramatically. "Mom, this isn't a wedding! Can't you just let me handle it?"

Temilola smirked, her tone unyielding. "There are plenty of girls your age who'd kill for a mom like me. Be grateful."

Priscilla slumped in defeat, recognizing that her mother's involvement was a non-negotiable clause. Any dreams of a wild, carefree party faded as Temilola turned to her breakfast with satisfaction.

A few nights later, during their usual mother-daughter movie ritual, Priscilla leaned into Temilola's side, her grin unmistakably mischievous.

"Mummy…" she began, her voice sing-song.

"Yes, dear?" Temilola replied distractedly, her eyes fixed on the screen.

Priscilla's grin widened as she asked, "So, who's your date for my birthday party?"

Temilola turned to her daughter, startled. "What date?" she managed, her composed demeanor faltering.

Priscilla batted her lashes innocently. "Well, I know you won't let me invite half the city. The least you can do is bring someone interesting for yourself."

"First of all," Temilola said, regaining her footing, "I'm too old to be anywhere near your party. Second, if you're planning another one of your ridiculous matchmaking stunts, forget it."

Priscilla laughed but said nothing, her fingers already hovering over her phone.

Temilola narrowed her eyes. "What you should be worrying about is giving me the guest list. Right now, there's no party to speak of—I haven't prepared anything."

Priscilla sighed, realizing her mom wasn't going to take the bait, and returned to her phone.

A few days later, Priscilla's best friend Afryea stopped by the penthouse to discuss the birthday party preparations. The two girls sprawled out in the living room, surrounded by a sea of magazines and color swatches, their conversation brimming with excitement.

"So, the theme is matching outfits," Priscilla declared, flipping through a bridal catalog for décor ideas. "Everyone has to bring a date, and couples need to coordinate their looks."

Afryea raised an eyebrow, smirking. "I hope you know that includes us. You *do* have a date, right?"

Priscilla groaned. "Don't remind me. I'll figure something out. What about you?"

Afryea hesitated, biting her lip. "Actually…" she trailed off, pulling out her phone. "I might have an idea, but it's a little... unconventional."

Before Priscilla could press her, Afryea dialed a number and held the phone to her ear.

"Who are you calling?" Priscilla whispered, leaning closer.

"My brother," Afryea mouthed.

On the other end, Jasper's familiar voice answered. "Afryea? What's up?"

Afryea rolled her eyes, trying to steady her voice. "Hey, Jasper. I need a favor."

Jasper chuckled knowingly. "This should be good. What kind of trouble are you in now?"

"I'm not in trouble!" Afryea snapped, though her cheeks flushed. "It's about Priscilla's birthday party. I need... well, I need you to be my date."

There was a brief silence before Jasper burst into laughter. "Wait, wait—*you* want me to be your date? This must be serious."

Afryea groaned, pressing a hand to her forehead. "Look, are you going to help me or not?"

Jasper's amusement didn't waver. "Alright, I'll do it," he said after a beat. "But only on one condition."

Afryea sighed. "What?"

"If I decide to charm one of your pretty friends, you're not allowed to interfere."

Afryea groaned again, glancing at Priscilla, who was stifling her own laughter. "Fine, whatever. Just don't ruin this for me."

Jasper's laughter echoed through the phone. "Deal. I'll see you at the party."

As she hung up, Afryea slumped back onto the couch, exhaling loudly.

"Well, that's sorted," she said, avoiding Priscilla's amused gaze.

Priscilla smirked. "So, your brother, huh? This party just got *very* interesting."

Afryea tossed a pillow at her in mock annoyance, but deep down, she couldn't shake the feeling that involving Jasper might complicate things more than she intended.

Unbeknownst to Temilola, Afryea's brother Jasper had admired her from afar for months. Though she'd seen him at a few events, she had no idea he was connected to Priscilla's best friend.

As the days ticked down to the party, Temilola busied herself with preparations, blissfully unaware of the storm of complications brewing beneath her roof.

Rebeccah Worship

Chapter 7: Curveballs and Silver Threads

The morning of Priscilla's birthday dawned with a golden haze spilling through the penthouse windows, painting everything with a glow of anticipation. Temilola stood in the expansive living room, watching the decorators finalize her vision. Lush floral arrangements in pastel tones framed the space, glittering chandeliers reflected light onto the elegant dining setup, and each detail whispered sophistication. She had meticulously planned this day to embody elegance and joy.

Priscilla breezed into the room, her energy electric. Dressed in a simple robe, her hair pinned back in preparation for her glam session, she twirled once in the open space. "It's perfect, Mom," she said, a rare sincerity softening her tone. "Exactly what I wanted."

Temilola arched an eyebrow. "And here I thought you'd complain it wasn't 'wild' enough."

Priscilla grinned sheepishly, her mother's comment hitting the mark. "I'm older now. Mature, even. Classy is good."

Temilola chuckled but said nothing, relieved her daughter was finally embracing the elegance she had worked so hard to cultivate.

By the time the party began, the penthouse brimmed with life. The hum of music, laughter, and chatter filled the space as impeccably dressed guests mingled. Temilola, in an emerald-green gown that accentuated her figure, moved through the crowd with poise. Her gracious smile charmed everyone she greeted, though a strange sense of anticipation buzzed at the edges of her consciousness.

Across the room, Priscilla sparkled in her sequined silver dress, chatting animatedly with Afryea, who had just arrived with Jasper in tow. Following their plan, Jasper and Afryea dressed as a couple—Jasper in a sleek black suit with a silver tie and Afryea in a matching silver jumpsuit.

Jasper, however, had motives of his own. The moment his eyes landed on Temilola, his breath caught. He recognized her instantly from the gym but seeing her now—radiant, commanding, surrounded by admirers—left him momentarily stunned. *Even more stunning than I remembered,* he thought, his usual confidence slipping.

Sensing his distraction, Afryea nudged him sharply. "Focus, Romeo. You're supposed to be my boyfriend tonight, not drooling over Priscilla's mom."

Jasper smirked, his composure returning. "Relax, little sis. I'm playing my part. For now."

Temilola moved effortlessly through the room, engaging with her guests. Her instincts, however, didn't fail to register the magnetic presence of a particular stranger. When Jasper finally approached her, it wasn't with hesitation but a quiet confidence that caught her off guard.

"Mrs. Adeniyi," he said smoothly, extending a hand. "It's a pleasure to finally meet you."

Temilola tilted her head, searching his face for familiarity. "I'm sorry, have we met?"

"Not formally," Jasper replied lightly. "But I've heard plenty about you from my sister, Afryea."

Realization dawned, and Temilola's guarded smile softened. "Ah, Afryea's brother. She's spoken of you, though I didn't expect to meet you under these circumstances."

"And I didn't expect you to be so…" Jasper paused, his gaze lingering a moment too long, "…intimidatingly beautiful."

Temilola blinked, caught off guard by his boldness. Before she could respond, Priscilla appeared at her side, her expression unreadable as her eyes darted between them. "Mom, Jasper! You've met!" she said, her tone too bright to be casual.

"Yes," Temilola replied, recovering her composure. "Your friend's brother was just introducing himself."

Priscilla's smile tightened, but she masked her suspicion well. "Well, don't let him bore you with his charm. Come, Mom, there's someone else I want you to meet."

Jasper chuckled softly as Priscilla whisked Temilola away. His gaze lingered on her retreating form, intrigued. Meanwhile, Temilola couldn't shake the strange fluttering sensation his words had left behind—a mix of intrigue and unease.

As the night drew to a close, guests filtered out with laughter and glowing compliments, leaving Temilola overseeing the cleanup. She stood by the window, nursing a glass of champagne, finally allowing herself a moment to breathe.

"Lovely evening," came a familiar voice behind her.

She turned to find Jasper, his tone softer now that the crowd had thinned. "Thank you for hosting such a wonderful event—and for tolerating my antics," he added, a faint smile playing on his lips.

Temilola gave a small, reserved smile. "It was nothing," she said simply.

Jasper hesitated, then took a step closer. "I'd like to see you again. Properly."

Temilola's heart skipped, but her voice remained calm. "Goodnight, Jasper."

Jasper's smile didn't falter as he inclined his head and walked away.

As the last of the evening faded into the city lights, Temilola stared out into the night. Her calm exterior belied the swirl of questions in her mind. Had fate just thrown her another curveball?

Rebeccah Worship

Chapter 8: Fateful Encounters on the High Seas

It had been a stellar quarter for Temilola's marketing firm, and the celebration matched the occasion: an exclusive yacht party for top clients and esteemed friends. The event, invitation-only, radiated sophistication and luxury. Temilola had expected the evening to be a showcase of professional success, surrounded by familiar faces from her elite client circle.

As she stepped onto the main deck, the sight took her breath away. The yacht gleamed under soft golden lights, and the air buzzed with an elegant energy. A live band played smooth highlife music that wove seamlessly into the hum of animated conversation. Guests, dressed in designer attire, sipped on aged wines and nibbled on decadent hors d'oeuvres. At the center of attention stood a dazzling ice sculpture of a whale, encircled by a lavish seafood display—a detail both extravagant and mesmerizing.

Dressed in a striking red gown that hugged her figure and commanded attention, Temilola moved toward the bar. Taking a seat with a glass of wine in hand, she allowed herself a rare moment to revel in the opulence of the evening. Her role as hostess was momentarily suspended, giving her time to absorb the beauty of the surroundings.

Then, her gaze snagged on a figure across the room, and her heart skipped a beat. Jasper.

This was the third time their paths had crossed—first at the gym, then at Priscilla's birthday party, and now here, at her firm's exclusive event. Temilola couldn't help but wonder: was this serendipity, or was the universe nudging her toward something she wasn't prepared to name?

Jasper stood near the center of the room, effortlessly commanding attention. Dressed in a double-breasted charcoal blazer with a satin red tie and silk accents, he exuded confidence. The tailored suit fit him like a glove, accentuating his broad shoulders and lean frame. Temilola's breath caught at the sight of him—his charm seemed to fill the room, drawing executives and glamorous women alike into his orbit.

She noticed him before he noticed her. While he regaled his companions with some witty remark, laughter rippling through the group, Temilola couldn't help but study him from her seat at the bar. Her attention lingered, her focus sharpening until she realized that others had begun to notice her unwavering gaze. Subtle whispers and curious glances swept the room, their hushed speculations only heightening her sense of vulnerability.

As if feeling the weight of her attention, Jasper's head turned, his eyes scanning the crowd until they locked onto hers. The intensity of his gaze sent a jolt through Temilola, her composure faltering under its weight. In a bid to recover, she turned back toward the bartender, feigning interest in the wine glass she held.

Get it together, she thought, taking a slow, steadying sip. She told herself that he would likely return to his group, dismissing her as just another guest. But as the seconds ticked by, her heart betrayed her, beating faster with each passing moment.

Then, she felt it—a subtle shift in the room's energy. The music softened, voices dimmed, and the air itself seemed to hold its breath.

He was behind her.

Slowly, Temilola turned.

Jasper stood towering over her, his presence magnetic and commanding. The soft lighting framed his chiseled features, sharpening his jawline and illuminating the faintest glimmer in his eyes. He leaned in just enough to close the distance, his voice a low, teasing whisper meant only for her ears.

"You seem to be causing a commotion."

Temilola's breath caught in her throat, a mix of thrill and embarrassment sparking through her. She managed to meet his gaze, though her carefully maintained poise threatened to crumble under the weight of his intensity.

"Is that so?" she replied, her voice steady but edged with intrigue.

Jasper's lips curved into a slight smile, the kind that hinted at secrets only he knew. "Definitely."

The moment stretched between them, charged with an unspoken electricity. The world around them seemed to blur, leaving only the two of them standing on the precipice of something extraordinary. Temilola's mind raced, but her heart seemed content to follow this uncharted path, wherever it might lead.

Whatever happened next, she knew one thing for certain: this encounter was no coincidence.

Chapter 9: The Edge of Control

Temilola composed herself quickly, summoning the practiced grace that had carried her through countless high-stakes meetings and glittering social events. She turned to face Jasper fully, her lips curving into a polite, albeit guarded, smile.

"Causing a commotion?" she echoed, her voice steady despite the flutter in her chest. "I think you might be exaggerating."

Jasper tilted his head slightly, the faintest smirk playing at the corner of his mouth. "Am I? You seemed pretty captivated back there."

He gestured casually toward the spot where she'd been sitting, his confidence unwavering.

Temilola raised an eyebrow, determined not to give him the upper hand. "Captivated? Hardly. Just surveying the crowd, as any good host would." She took a deliberate sip of her wine, using the pause to gather her thoughts.

"You're the host?" Jasper asked, his curiosity piqued. "Now I'm even more impressed."

Temilola glanced at him, her expression a mix of intrigue and caution. "I see you've found your way into quite an exclusive circle tonight. Should I assume you're here on business or pleasure?"

Jasper chuckled, a low, rich sound that seemed to ripple through the air between them. "A little of both. One of my investors insisted I attend—he's a big fan of yours, by the way."

"Smart investor," Temilola quipped, a flicker of amusement crossing her face. "Though I'm surprised you didn't mention you were in business yourself. Afryea certainly never said anything about that."

Jasper shrugged, the movement easy and unbothered. "Afryea tends to keep me out of her stories. Can't say I blame her—it's probably easier to pretend I'm just her annoying older brother." His tone was light, but his gaze was sharp, searching hers for a reaction.

Temilola allowed herself a small laugh. "Well, you do seem to have a knack for showing up unexpectedly. First the gym, then Priscilla's party, and now here."

"Some might call it fate," Jasper said, his voice softening as he leaned in just a fraction closer. "Or maybe just good timing."

Temilola felt a flicker of heat rise to her cheeks, but she maintained her composure. "Timing can be a tricky thing," she replied, her tone even. "Especially when there's an audience."

Jasper glanced around, as if noticing for the first time the curious stares and murmured conversations rippling through the room. "Ah," he said with a grin. "They're just jealous they're not the ones talking to you."

Temilola shook her head, laughing softly despite herself. "You're incorrigible."

"And you're avoiding the question," Jasper countered, his eyes gleaming with mischief. "Would you let me steal you away for a moment? I promise not to keep you too long."

Temilola hesitated, the weight of their previous encounters and the potential implications of this moment pressing against her thoughts. She glanced toward the crowd, a sea of influential faces that had come to see her as the composed, untouchable professional.

But something in Jasper's presence—his quiet confidence, the ease with which he stood against the backdrop of power and prestige—made her pause. For once, she wondered what it might feel like to step out of her carefully constructed image, even for just a moment.

With a deep breath, she set her glass down on the bar and met his gaze. "Alright, Mr. Good Timing," she said, her voice laced with a hint of challenge. "Let's see what you've got."

Jasper's smile widened, and he extended a hand toward her. As she placed hers in his, the warmth of his touch sent a subtle thrill through her. Together, they moved away from the bar, the buzz of the room fading into the background.

Temilola followed Jasper out to the open-air deck at the rear of the yacht. The Lagos skyline glimmered in the distance, the city's vibrant chaos muted by the soft, rhythmic swaddle of waves against the hull. A gentle breeze swept over them, carrying the mingling scents of saltwater and jasmine from the floral arrangements scattered throughout the deck.

Jasper led her to a quieter corner, away from the crowd but still within view of the party's glow. The live band's melodies drifted out here, more subdued, a subtle soundtrack to the charged silence between them.

"Quite the setting," Jasper remarked, leaning casually against the railing. His voice, low and smooth, carried an undertone that sent a shiver through Temilola. "You have a talent for curating perfection."

"Only the best for my clients," she replied, her tone clipped but not cold. Her professional mask was slipping, and she felt it. Something about Jasper's presence made it hard to maintain the usual distance she kept with men who showed interest in her.

Jasper smiled knowingly, his gaze never leaving hers. "And for yourself?"

Temilola hesitated, the question catching her off guard. "What do you mean?"

"Do you ever curate perfection just for you?" he asked, stepping closer, his voice dropping into something more intimate. The space between them shrank, the air thickening with unspoken possibilities.

The challenge in his words stirred something rebellious in her. "I find joy in the work I do. Isn't that enough?"

"Joy," Jasper repeated, his lips curving into a slight smirk. "Is that what you call it?"

Temilola opened her mouth to respond, but the words caught in her throat. Jasper had stepped closer still, close enough that the heat of his body seemed to envelop her. Her heart raced, and she hated how transparent it felt in this moment. Her pulse betrayed her, pounding loudly in her ears as he leaned in.

His hand, warm and steady, brushed lightly against hers on the railing. The touch was electric, a whisper of contact that sent a ripple through her. She should have stepped back. Every logical part of her screamed to retreat, to reassert the boundaries she so carefully maintained. And yet, she didn't move.

"You're used to control," Jasper murmured, his face now inches from hers. His voice was so soft it barely carried over the sound of the waves. "But sometimes, it's worth letting go."

Her breath hitched as his words hung between them, daring her to cross the line. His eyes searched hers, not with arrogance but with a confidence that told her he was unafraid of whatever answer she might give.

"Mrs. Adeniyi!"

The interruption shattered the moment like glass. Temilola flinched, instinctively stepping back, her hand slipping from the railing. Chief Adetokunbo, one of her longest-standing clients, approached with a jovial grin, his voice booming across the deck.

Temilola pivoted smoothly, her professional mask snapping into place. The weight of Jasper's gaze lingered on her back as she exchanged pleasantries with the Chief.

When the Chief moved on, Jasper leaned in once more. "Saved by the Chief," he murmured. "Lucky for you—or unlucky?"

Temilola's lips curved into a faint smile. "Maybe both," she replied, her tone cool, though her heart still raced.

She turned back toward the crowd, retreating to the safety of her well-crafted world, but her thoughts remained on the man who had so effortlessly unraveled her composure.

Rebeccah Worship

Chapter 10: A Line in the Sand

As Temilola mingled with the crowd, her outward composure was flawless. To the world, she was the picture of poise—a radiant hostess commanding the room. But inside, her thoughts clashed like storm-tossed waves, each one pulling her further into uncertainty. She clutched her wine glass tightly, the delicate stem a fragile tether to reality, and let her practiced smile guide her through the polite chatter.

The laughter, the clinking of glasses, and the smooth melodies of the live band blurred into background noise as her mind drifted back to Jasper. What had she been thinking? Allowing herself to be so affected by someone nearly half her age? It wasn't just his boldness or the easy charm he wore like a second skin— it was the way he made her feel. Seen. Desired. For the first time in years, she wasn't just the sharp, polished professional who ruled her world with an iron will.

But that was precisely the problem. How could someone so young understand her complexities, her battles, her sacrifices? Jasper's youthful confidence stood in stark contrast to the battle-worn armor she had forged through years of struggle and sacrifice. Could he truly grasp the weight of her scars, or was he destined to remain a fleeting distraction—a reminder of a freedom she no longer dared to embrace?

A fresh wave of guilt hit her as her thoughts turned to Priscilla. Her daughter was her everything—her greatest accomplishment, the reason she had rebuilt her life after it had shattered. Temilola had worked tirelessly to be a mother her daughter could admire strong, disciplined, grounded. Yet here she was, shaken by a man whose audacity to approach her should have been laughable.

But it wasn't laughable. It was thrilling.

Her fingers tightened around the wine glass as she replayed the moment on the yacht's deck. Jasper's gaze had been intense, his touch warm, his words a heady mix of sincerity and flirtation. He had drawn closer, his presence magnetic, as though the world around them had ceased to exist. She hadn't felt that alive in years—and that terrified her.

"Mrs. Adeniyi?"

The voice snapped her back to the present. One of her junior associates stood before her, looking expectantly at her, evidently waiting for an answer to a question she hadn't even registered.

"Yes, of course," she replied smoothly, masking her inner turmoil with a gracious smile. The associate seemed satisfied and continued talking, but Temilola's attention was already drifting again.

Her eyes found Jasper across the room. He stood near the bar, surrounded by a group of men, his posture relaxed, and his gestures animated. His laughter—a deep, rumbling sound she could almost hear from where she stood—seemed to captivate everyone around him. It was effortless for him, this magnetic pull he had on people. On her.

A flicker of irritation rose within her. She wasn't some naive girl to be swept away by a charming smile and a well-fitted suit. She was Temilola Adeniyi—CEO, mother, survivor. She had built an empire with her bare hands and had no time for frivolities. And yet, here she was, stealing glances at a man she had no business entertaining.

Her chest tightened as guilt and longing tangled into a knot she couldn't untangle. This can't happen, she told herself firmly. It's not just the age—it's the implications. The judgments. The risks. And beneath all of that was a deeper fear that whispered: What if I get hurt again?

Determined to regain control, she turned her gaze away. This wasn't just about her. There was Priscilla to consider, her hard-earned reputation, and the delicate line she walked as a woman of power in a society that scrutinized her every move. She couldn't afford to let a fleeting attraction unravel the life she had worked so hard to rebuild.

Yet, even as she resolved to put Jasper out of her mind, her traitorous heart clung to the memory of his whispered words and the way they had made her feel.

The evening's festivities wound down, but the storm inside Temilola only grew stronger. As her driver maneuvered through Lagos's glittering night streets, she leaned her head against the cool glass of the window, hoping it might steady her. But her thoughts refused to settle.

Jasper's presence lingered, an unshakable shadow in her mind. The way he had looked at her—like she was the only person in the room—played on a loop. She couldn't deny it anymore: she was deeply, almost dangerously, attracted to him. That realization sent a jolt of both excitement and apprehension through her. What am I doing? she thought, her fingers absently toying with the strap of her clutch.

By the time they arrived at her penthouse, the question remained unanswered. She stepped out of the car, thanking the driver softly, and entered her home—a comforting blend of sleek minimalism and warmth.

Priscilla was already home, lounging on the oversized sectional with a tub of ice cream balanced on her lap.

"Hey, Mom," Priscilla called, looking up from the romantic drama she was half-watching, half-scrolling through on her phone. "How was the yacht party? Did you 'network' or whatever it is you do?"

Temilola dropped her clutch on the console table and slipped off her heels. She moved toward the couch and sank into the cushion beside her daughter. For a moment, she said nothing, searching for the right words to broach the thoughts swirling in her mind without giving too much away.

"It was nice," she replied finally, her voice measured. "Very elegant."

Priscilla raised a skeptical eyebrow. "That's your polite way of saying boring."

Temilola chuckled softly. "Not entirely. There was... someone interesting there."

Priscilla's attention snapped to her at once, her eyes lighting up with mischief. "Someone interesting?" she repeated, dragging out the words. "Mom, are you trying to tell me you met someone?"

Temilola immediately regretted her phrasing. "No," she said quickly, too quickly. "Not like that. I just meant... he stood out."

Priscilla smirked, clearly unconvinced. "Oh, so it is a 'he.'" She leaned forward, her grin widening. "Okay, spill. What's his deal? Is he handsome? Rich? Mysterious?"

"None of your business," Temilola said firmly, though her cheeks betrayed her with the faintest flush.

Priscilla laughed, leaning back and licking her spoon. "Fine, fine. Be all cryptic. But for the record, I think it's great if you're putting yourself out there. You deserve to have some fun."

Temilola hesitated, emboldened by her daughter's casual encouragement. She leaned slightly closer, her voice dropping to a conspiratorial tone. "Hypothetically speaking, what would you think if I, say… dated someone closer to your age?"

Priscilla froze mid-bite, staring at her mother with wide eyes. Then, after a long pause, she burst into uncontrollable laughter.

"Oh my God, Mom," she wheezed, clutching her stomach. "That's the funniest thing you've ever said. Next thing, you'll tell me you're joining my gym to pick up guys."

Temilola forced a laugh, masking the awkwardness creeping in. "I'm glad you think I have a future in comedy," she said dryly, leaning back into the couch.

Priscilla shook her head, still chuckling as she resumed scrolling. "Seriously, though. Imagine you showing up at my birthday party with the guy I went to school with."

"Imagine," Temilola echoed softly, her thoughts turning inward.

As her daughter's laughter faded into the background, Temilola's mind wandered back to the yacht. For a brief moment, Jasper had made her feel like a woman again—not a mother, not a CEO, but someone desirable and desired.

And yet, here was Priscilla, laughing off the very idea. Perhaps the universe wasn't mocking her but protecting her, drawing a firm line in the sand. Whatever spark had flickered between them was never meant to ignite. And yet, as the night deepened, Temilola couldn't help but wonder—what if some lines weren't meant to be obeyed?

Chapter 11: A Gift in Gold and Flame

Two weeks had passed since the unforgettable encounter on the yacht. Although Jasper hadn't secured Temilola's phone number, he knew finding her contact details wouldn't be an issue. Yet, uncertainty gnawed at him.

"Was I too forward? Did I mess things up? Or... maybe she's just not interested?" he wondered aloud, pacing his apartment. Frustration mounted as the silence stretched. "Should I call her? No—too late now. I've waited too long," he muttered, running a hand through his hair. "I need to do something...

something subtle but meaningful. She needs to know she's been on my mind."

Resolved, Jasper got dressed and left his apartment. Hours later, he returned with a sleek, luxurious gift box in hand, its wrapping crisp and elegant. On the label, a single instruction: *"For work. Please open privately."*

He turned to his sister, Afryea, to ensure its safe delivery. "Here's the deal," he began, holding out the box. "If you hand-deliver this to Temilola—personally—I'll get you two VIP passes with backstage access to the next Davido concert."

Afryea's eyes lit up, though Jasper wasn't done. "And don't breathe a word about the passes to Priscilla until I've secured them. Got it?"

Afryea nodded eagerly, already envisioning herself backstage. "Deal!" she exclaimed, clutching the box tightly as she plotted her delivery strategy.

At her penthouse, Temilola tried to maintain her work-life boundaries, but the yacht event she had organized for her company had left her playing catch-up. Deadlines loomed, and she reluctantly worked from her home office one evening.

She was drafting an email when her phone buzzed. Seeing the name Jasmine, a smile broke across her face.

Jasmine had joined Temilola's company three years ago to spearhead U.S. customer acquisition. What began as a professional relationship blossomed into a deep friendship. But Jasmine's move to a better job in the U.S. had separated them. Though they stayed in touch, it had been nearly a year since they'd seen each other.

Jasmine's call was a welcome break, and her cheerful reminder of her arrival the next evening left Temilola excited—and suddenly aware of the preparations needed.

The moment the call ended, she dashed downstairs. "Priscilla! Priscilla!" she called.

Priscilla, startled by her mother's urgency, glanced up from her phone. "What's wrong, Mom?"

Temilola waved a hand dismissively. "Do you remember Jasmine?"

Before Priscilla could answer, the front door opened. Afryea entered, a box in her hands. "Hi, Aunty!" she greeted warmly.

Priscilla's attention shifted immediately. "What's with the box?"

Temilola, irritated, snapped, "Priscilla, focus! I'm talking to you!"

Priscilla flinched. "Sorry, Mom," she replied, though her eyes returned to the box. "Is it a surprise gift for me?"

"It's not for you," Afryea said firmly, clutching the box tighter.

"If it's not for Priscilla, then what's in it?" Temilola asked, her curiosity piqued.

"It's for you!" Afryea blurted, unable to contain her excitement.

"For me? Why?"

Afryea couldn't hold back anymore. "Because me and my bestie, Priscilla, are going to see Davido live—WITH BACKSTAGE PASSES!" she squealed, jumping up and down.

Before the box could meet an untimely demise in her enthusiasm, Temilola took it. She noticed the label: *"For work. Please open privately."*

Her curiosity deepened. Without another word, she ascended the stairs, the box securely under her arm.

In her room, Temilola shut the door firmly and placed the box on her vanity. The label's instruction repeated in her mind. Was this from a client? A secret admirer? Jasper?

The last thought made her pulse quicken, but she quickly dismissed it. No, it couldn't be.

She unwrapped the box, revealing a luxurious leather-bound planner embossed with her initials in gold. Beside it lay a gold pen engraved with the words: *"For the woman who commands every room she enters."*

Her breath caught. Then she noticed a folded parchment tucked inside. She unfolded it carefully, revealing bold handwriting in black ink.

"Temilola,
You don't just enter a room; you consume it, making everything and everyone around you burn brighter."

The words gripped her, pulling her into the letter.

"I haven't stopped thinking about the way you looked that night on the yacht. That red dress—it was as though the stars themselves envied your radiance. But it wasn't just how you looked; it was how you carried yourself. You had me spellbound long before you turned around and saw me.

Do you remember how close we were on the deck? The scent of the ocean mingling with your perfume, the way the world around us blurred until it was just you and me? I've replayed that moment countless times—the softness of your voice, the spark in your eyes.

You are strength and elegance personified, but what draws me to you most is the fire beneath the surface. I want to know that fire intimately, to stoke it, to be consumed by it.

This letter may be bold, but so was every step I took toward you that night. Every step since has been guided by the thought of you. If you feel even a fraction of what I do, then tell me. Let me know there's a chance for this flame to grow."

Yours,

Jasper"

Temilola's hands trembled as she lowered the letter. The memories Jasper described flooded back with startling clarity—the red dress, the ocean breeze, the charged silence.

Her heart wavered. The raw honesty in his words left her feeling desired and deeply seen. Yet guilt gnawed at her. Could she entertain this?

Her fingers lingered over his name as emotions warred within her—desire, hesitation, and the fear of stepping into the unknown.

Chapter 12: Crossroads of the Heart

After a grueling day at work, Temilola raced to the airport to pick up Jasmine. Despite leaving early to avoid Lagos' notorious traffic, she found herself stuck in a sea of honking cars and frustrated drivers. Thankfully, Jasmine's flight was delayed, granting Temilola just enough time to arrive at the airport before her best friend emerged from the terminal.

The arrivals area buzzed with activity as Temilola scanned the crowd, searching for Jasmine. Her heart skipped a beat when she heard a familiar voice shouting, "Temi! Temi!" She turned, her eyes widening as she spotted

Jasmine, a striking figure in a chic pink double-breasted suit, her designer heels clicking confidently against the tile floor.

"Jasmine!" Temilola exclaimed, laughing as her friend charged through the crowd with dramatic flair, drawing amused stares.

Jasmine threw her arms around Temilola in a tight embrace. "Oh my God, Temi! I missed you so much!" she gushed, ignoring the onlookers.

Temilola laughed, shaking her head. "You're impossible. This is Lagos, Jasmine. You can't just act like this is a Broadway stage!"

Jasmine pulled back, grinning. "Who cares? It's you! I had to make an entrance."

"You certainly did," Temilola replied, her voice tinged with amusement. "Come on, let's get your bags and head home before your 'entrance' attracts more attention."

When they arrived at the penthouse, upbeat music echoed from the living room. There, Priscilla and Afryea were immersed in their dance rehearsal for Davido's concert, their moves perfectly synchronized with the music video playing on the screen.

"Priscilla!" Jasmine called, striding into the room with open arms.

Priscilla turned, her face lighting up. "Jasmine! I remember you!" she said, rushing to embrace her.

"This is the friend I was trying to tell you about before Afryea showed up with that fancy box," Temilola interjected, rolling her eyes for emphasis.

"Haa, I see…" Priscilla replied, her voice dripping with mock understanding. "And what's this about a fancy box?"

"Oh, don't start!" Temilola said, waving her off. "Jasmine, let's get you settled."

That night, the two old friends stayed up late, chatting in Temilola's room like they used to during their youth. Jasmine's laughter filled the space, her wit as sharp as ever. Eventually, the conversation shifted to Jasper.

"So," Jasmine said, her tone sly. "Tell me about this mysterious box—and the man behind it."

Temilola hesitated, her smile faltering. "It's complicated."

Jasmine raised an eyebrow. "Complicated is my favorite kind. Spill."

Temilola sighed, brushing her fingers against her silk blouse. "He's younger. Much younger."

"How much younger are we talking?" Jasmine leaned in, her curiosity piqued. "Ten years? Fifteen?"

"Closer to Priscilla's age," Temilola admitted, bracing for her friend's reaction.

Jasmine's jaw dropped. "Temi! You're serious?" she exclaimed, her laughter bubbling out. "Miss Dior Heels is into someone barely out of his twenties?"

"He's not a boy," Temilola said sharply, surprising them both with her intensity.

Jasmine sobered, studying her friend closely. "You're serious," she said softly.

"I didn't plan for this," Temilola said, her voice quieter. "But he's... magnetic. When he looks at me, it's like I'm the only woman in the room. It's overwhelming."

Jasmine softened. "Okay, so it's not just some fleeting crush. But what's stopping you? The age gap?"

"Partly," Temilola admitted. "But mostly, it's... how people will see it. I don't want to be judged, especially by Priscilla."

Jasmine leaned forward, her expression thoughtful. "Temi, when you're with him—or thinking about him—does it feel wrong? Or does it make you feel alive?"

Temilola looked down, her fingers tracing the rim of her coffee mug. "Alive," she whispered.

"Then maybe it's time to stop caring about what everyone else thinks," Jasmine said gently. "Life's too short for regrets."

Before Temilola could respond, Priscilla's voice echoed from the hallway. "Mom, Jasmine! Breakfast is ready!"

"Saved by the bell," Temilola muttered, earning a chuckle from Jasmine.

"This conversation isn't over," Jasmine teased as they made their way to the dining room. But even as they joined Priscilla and Afryea at the table, Jasmine's words lingered in Temilola's mind, stirring questions she wasn't yet ready to answer.

Chapter 13: Unveiled Intentions

One of Temilola's most prominent clients, Mrs. Ajayi, personally delivered an elegant envelope containing an invitation to her son Dayo's 30th birthday party. Both Temilola and her daughter, Priscilla, were invited. Temilola was taken aback. While she was confident her clients admired her, she couldn't shake the feeling that the invitation might be more about her 23-year-old daughter than her. Counting down the minutes until the end of her workday, she couldn't wait to share the news with Jasmine over the phone.

"Girl! I don't even know what this means. Is this invitation for me or my daughter? I mean, she knows I'm single, but I'm almost 15 years older than her son!" Temilola vented, embarrassment evident in her voice.

"Relax," Jasmine replied with a laugh. "That smart lady is playing matchmaker, trying to kill two birds with one stone. Don't overthink it. Let's go, drink some expensive wine, and mingle with rich men. It'll be fun!"

Later that evening, Temilola announced a shopping trip to Priscilla and Afryea without revealing the true reason. Since Afryea wasn't invited to the party, she framed it as a casual outing. They spent the day laughing, snacking, and shopping, but Temilola made sure to secure stunning outfits for herself, Priscilla, and Jasmine for the upcoming event.

When the weekend arrived, the party turned out to be an opulent affair. The venue, with its grand Victorian-style décor, glistened under soft lighting, while a live band played Afrobeat hits with a highlife twist. The menu featured a blend of familiar comfort foods and delicacies like Nkwobi. The guest list was a who's who of influential personalities.

"OMG, Jasmine, this place is buzzing with prospects!" Temilola whispered, her eyes wide with excitement.

"Damn, Mrs. Ajayi does not play! This woman is rich. This crowd is full of high-level officials. NEVER miss anything she invites you to," Jasmine replied, barely able to contain her excitement.

As they were chatting, Mrs. Ajayi approached, arms open for Temilola.

"I'm so glad you and your daughter could make it," she said warmly, kissing Temilola on both cheeks.

"Good evening, Mrs. Ajayi. The party is beautiful," Priscilla chimed in, stepping forward to hug her and diffuse any awkwardness.

"You look stunning in that yellow dress, Priscilla," Mrs. Ajayi complimented. "Let me introduce you to someone, if that's alright?" she said, glancing at Temilola for approval.

"Yes, of course!" Temilola replied, startled but eager to oblige. As Mrs. Ajayi led Priscilla away, Temilola and Jasmine exchanged giddy looks before sauntering toward the bar.

At the bar, Temilola playfully slammed her hand on the counter. "Two of your finest wines, please!" she declared, making the bartender chuckle as he poured two glasses of sweet red wine.

They were about to take their first sips when a familiar scent of expensive cologne enveloped Temilola. A smooth voice murmured, "I see you everywhere, beautiful lady."

Temilola froze, her breath catching. She turned slowly to meet Jasper's intense gaze. Dressed impeccably in a chocolate double-breasted suit with gold accents, he exuded effortless charm.

"Jasper," she managed, her voice barely above a whisper.

Their connection crackled in the air until Jasper's assistant, Tessy, interrupted hesitantly. "Sir, Honorable Abiola is requesting to see you."

"Now?" Jasper asked, visibly annoyed.

"Yes, sir."

Jasper sighed, his eyes still locked on Temilola. Fighting the urge to kiss her, he whispered, "Can I call you later?"

"Yes," she replied softly, lowering her gaze.

As Jasper walked off, Temilola remained rooted, her pulse racing.

"Earth to Temilola!" Jasmine teased, snapping her fingers in front of her friend's face.

Temilola fanned herself, laughing nervously. "Is it hot in here?"

"If by 'hot,' you mean that man who was just all over you—then yes. Now spill!" Jasmine demanded.

Before Temilola could respond, Jasper returned, only to overhear her whisper, "It's nothing. He's too young. This won't work."

His expression darkened. Without a word, he turned and headed to the balcony.

Realizing her mistake, Temilola called after him, "Jasper! Wait!" She followed him outside, finding him leaning on the railing.

"Jasper," she said gently, stepping closer. "It's not what you think."

He turned slowly, sadness clouding his eyes. "My age," he whispered, gripping her arms. "It always comes back to that."

Inside, Priscilla approached Jasmine. "Where's my mom?"

"Why are you looking for her? You're at a party—go mingle!" Jasmine replied, trying to deflect.

"What fun? This isn't a party; it's a networking event. And don't even get me started on Dayo. His mom's been parading him around all night like a prized cow!"

Jasmine burst into laughter, but Priscilla wasn't amused. Hearing her mother's voice from the balcony, she walked off to investigate.

On the balcony, Temilola tried to explain her hesitations, referencing past relationships and fears. Just as the tension softened, Priscilla burst through the door.

"What's going on here?" she asked, her gaze darting between her mother and Jasper.

"We're done here. Let's go," Priscilla declared, grabbing her mother's hand and pulling her away.

"I'm sorry, Jasper," Temilola said softly. "I have to go."

"I understand," he replied, his voice heavy with disappointment.

In the car, Priscilla ranted about Dayo. "How can a 30-year-old man have his mom throw him a birthday party? What's next, naming his pets?!"

Back at the penthouse, Temilola's phone buzzed. It was Jasper.

"I'd like to talk about what happened earlier... if that's okay. Can I take you on a proper date tomorrow evening?"

Temilola's heart fluttered. "I'd like that," she replied softly.

As she hung up, Priscilla and Jasmine stared at her curiously.

"Who was that?" Priscilla asked, shocked by her mom's girlish grin.

Before Temilola could respond, Jasmine intervened. "Your mom has a busy day tomorrow. Let's talk another time."

With a playful shove, Jasmine nudged Temilola upstairs, leaving Priscilla to puzzle over the sudden shift.

Chapter 14: Unraveled Expectations

The next evening arrived, bringing a wave of nervous anticipation for Temilola. She stood in front of her bedroom mirror, adjusting the folds of her off-shoulder dark green sequin dress-shirt. Paired with solid gold jewelry, a gold clutch, and nude, fluffy open-toe strap-on heels, her look exuded effortless elegance. Taking a deep breath, she sashayed playfully down the staircase, outwardly confident despite her inner turmoil.

Jasmine, waiting in the living room, lit up at the sight of her. But before she could speak, Priscilla beat her to it.

"Wow, you look amazing for a Sunday evening. What's the occasion, lady?" Priscilla teased, though a hint of curiosity colored her tone.

"She's going on a date!" Jasmine blurted out excitedly, forgetting that Temilola hadn't yet shared this news with Priscilla.

"A date? With whom? When?" Priscilla asked, her playful demeanor giving way to intrigue.

Temilola's radiant smile faltered. She realized the moment she'd dreaded was here—explaining her situation to Priscilla. With Jasper just minutes away, she knew she couldn't stall any longer.

"Priscilla, I need to tell you something. Come have a seat," Temilola said, gesturing toward the sofa.

Priscilla's smile vanished, replaced by a look of concern. "Okay… why do you look like that? What's going on?"

Taking a deep breath, Temilola braced herself. "Priscilla, I'm going on a date, and… you might not be thrilled when you hear who it's with," she admitted hesitantly.

"Just get to the point. This suspense is unnecessary," Jasmine quipped, rolling her eyes.

"Who is it?" Priscilla asked impatiently.

Temilola closed her eyes, her voice soft. "Jasper."

The room fell silent. Temilola peeked through one eye, expecting an explosion. At first, there was nothing, and she began to think she might have dodged a bullet.

"Well," she ventured, "I guess you're managing this better than I—"

"What the **FUCK?!**" Priscilla exploded, cutting her off.

"Watch your mouth!" Temilola and Jasmine scolded in unison.

"Okay, okay, I'm sorry. But Jasper? Afryea's older brother?" Priscilla demanded, clearly upset. "He's in his mid- to late-20s, Mom! I'm 23, and you're about to turn 45. Shouldn't I be the one dating him?"

Before Temilola could respond, the front door opened. Jasper stepped in, as instructed, only to find himself at the center of a storm. His gaze moved between Temilola, stunning yet distressed, and Priscilla, visibly upset.

"What's going on?" he asked, walking over to Temilola to give her a gentle hug.

Jasmine, ever quick-witted, rose and extended her hand. "I'm Jasmine," she introduced herself with a polite smile, eager to cut through the tension. Turning to Jasper, she continued, "Sorry you had to walk in on this, but Temilola just told Priscilla about your date, and… she's not handling it very well."

Jasper's expression hardened slightly, sensing the night teetering on the edge of disaster. Determined to take control, he made a bold move.

Without a word, Jasper stepped forward, took Temilola's hand, grabbed her clutch from the center table, and led her out of the penthouse.

Still stunned by Priscilla's outburst, Temilola followed in silence. Once in Jasper's car, she stared out the window, her thoughts racing. Jasper, gripping the steering wheel tightly, glanced at her occasionally, his mind racing to salvage the evening.

He thought about the weeks they'd spent getting to know each other, the barriers Temilola had carefully erected, and the delicate moments when he saw glimpses of the real her.

Tonight, he resolved, I'll find a way to make her smile again. And maybe, just maybe, this will be the night I finally get that kiss—it's been two months of waiting too long.

Rebeccah Worship

Chapter 15: Unraveled and Reborn

The tension in the car was palpable. Temilola's thoughts churned with worry over Priscilla's reaction, but the warmth of Jasper's hand resting lightly on hers as he navigated the bustling Lagos streets grounded her. His touch was steady, reassuring—reminding her why she'd allowed herself to entertain this connection despite the odds.

"Are you okay?" Jasper finally asked, his deep voice breaking the silence.

Temilola turned to him, her lips curving into a faint smile. "I don't know. Priscilla's reaction was… intense, but I can't blame her. This is a lot to take in."

Jasper nodded, his gaze fixed on the road. "I get it. She's protective of you, and the situation is unconventional. But I'm not going anywhere, Temilola. I want us to figure this out—together."

His words hung in the air, soothing some of the storm within her. She shifted in her seat, allowing herself to relax slightly. "Where are we going?" she asked, eager to change the subject.

Jasper smirked, his dimple making a brief appearance. "It's a surprise. Trust me."

Temilola raised a skeptical brow but didn't press further. Soon, the car pulled up to a secluded rooftop restaurant overlooking the city. Soft fairy lights framed the edges of the space, and the mellow hum of live jazz music greeted them as they stepped out. The setting was intimate and romantic, a stark contrast to the chaos she'd left behind.

"Wow," Temilola whispered, taking in the breathtaking view of Lagos, the city lights twinkling like stars. "This is beautiful."

"I thought you deserved something special," Jasper replied, guiding her toward a private table set with candles and fresh flowers. "After everything, I wanted tonight to be about you."

Temilola felt a warmth spread through her chest. It wasn't just the setting—it was the way Jasper looked at her, as though she were the only person in the world. For a moment, all her doubts melted away.

As the evening unfolded, they talked about everything—his ambitions, her fears, and their shared love for travel. Jasper had a knack for making her laugh, easing the tension on her shoulders with every witty remark and charming smile. They shared a bottle of fine red wine, their glasses clinking in silent celebration of the moment.

"Why me, Jasper?" Temilola asked suddenly, her voice softer now, her curiosity genuine. "You could have anyone. Someone closer to your age, someone without the baggage."

Jasper leaned back in his chair, studying her. "Because you're different, Temi. You're intelligent, graceful, and unapologetically yourself. You make me want to be better, and when I'm with you, everything feels… right."

Her cheeks flushed at his honesty. She was about to respond when the waiter arrived with dessert—an intricately plated chocolate fondant with a scoop of vanilla gelato. Jasper leaned forward, slicing a piece and offering her the first bite.

"Careful," he teased. "It's hot."

She accepted the gesture, savoring the rich, velvety flavor. "Mmm," she murmured, closing her eyes briefly. "This might just be the best thing I've tasted all year."

Jasper laughed, his eyes sparkling. "Good to know I'm second-best."

Temilola playfully smacked his arm, her laughter genuine. For the first time in weeks, she felt at ease. As the night wound down, they stood by the railing, gazing out at the city. The cool breeze tugged at her curls, and she shivered slightly. Jasper immediately draped his suit jacket over her shoulders, his hands lingering on her arms.

"Temi," he began, his voice low, "I've been wanting to do this for a while now."

Before she could ask what he meant, he closed the space between them, his lips brushing hers in a soft, deliberate kiss. Time seemed to stand still as she let herself lean into him, the world around them fading away.

When they finally pulled apart, Jasper's forehead rested against hers, his smile tender. "I've been waiting for that moment since the day I met you."

Temilola laughed softly, her heart racing.

"It was worth the wait."

Chapter 16: A Kaleidoscope of Choices

The city lights blurred into a kaleidoscope as Temilola and Jasper stepped out of the restaurant, their laughter softening the weight of years and unsaid emotions lingering between them. The crisp night air kissed her skin, carrying the faint promise of rain.

Her heel caught on the uneven cobblestones, a betrayal after too much merlot. Jasper's hand shot out instinctively, steadying her with a firm, reassuring grip. His warmth seeped into her skin, and when their eyes met, the world tilted—not from the wine but from the intensity of his gaze. His stormy eyes held her captive, searching for something unspoken.

"You okay?" he asked, his voice lower now, rough around the edges.

"Yeah," she whispered, suddenly aware of how close they were. The faint scent of his cologne mixed with the cool night air, wrapping around her like a cocoon.

The city hummed around them—cars in the distance, faint chatter from passersby—but here, in this fragile bubble, the universe seemed to pause.

Jasper leaned in slowly, deliberately, as though giving her time to pull away. His lips brushed hers softly, tentative yet electric. When she didn't retreat—instead lifting her hands to rest on his chest—the kiss deepened. Years of restraint dissolved in that single, fervent moment.

Temilola felt like she was free-falling, and for once, she didn't care. Jasper's hand cradled her jaw, his touch reverent, as though she were something fragile yet vital. When they finally broke apart, her breath came in uneven gasps, her lips tingling from the intensity.

"I shouldn't drive," he admitted, his voice hoarse, almost apologetic. "I've had too much."

Going home wasn't an option—not tonight, not with Priscilla waiting to dissect her every move. "Then let's go somewhere," she said, the words tumbling out before she could second-guess herself. "A hotel."

The hotel room was intimate and tastefully furnished, bathed in the soft amber glow of a bedside lamp. Temilola stood by the window, staring out at the city lights, her heart racing.

Jasper approached cautiously, his movements unhurried, his voice a gentle murmur. "Are you sure about this?"

Turning to face him, she saw the vulnerability in his expression, a crack in the confident facade she'd always known. "Yes," she said, her voice steady despite the storm inside. "I don't want to think tonight. I just want to feel."

His hand cupped her cheek, his thumb brushing her skin in a tender caress. "If you want to stop—"

"I'll tell you," she assured him, her lips curving into a soft, grateful smile.

The kiss that followed was different— deeper, more certain. Hands explored, fabric fell away, and the space between them evaporated. Their movements were unhurried yet charged, a deliberate dance that unfolded with aching tenderness.

When they finally came together, the world outside faded entirely. Each shared breath, every whispered name, spoke of something beyond physical desire—something raw and profound. Their connection surged like waves meeting the shore, a rhythm as natural as it was undeniable.

Temilola shattered first, the intensity overwhelming, her cries mingling with Jasper's guttural groan as he followed her into the abyss. In the stillness that followed, they lay entwined, their bodies humming with aftershocks, their hearts beating in quiet unison.

Morning crept in softly, and Jasper, ever the early riser, orchestrated a breakfast that rivaled a feast. By the time Temilola stirred, the room was filled with the aroma of fresh pastries and savory delicacies.

Blinking groggily, her gaze landed on the table laden with an extravagant spread: bagels, waffles, akara, fried chicken, suya, and more. She stared, stunned by the abundance, before her eyes found Jasper, shirtless and relaxed on the bed.

"I didn't know what you'd like, so I got everything," he said with a teasing grin.

"Hmmm," she murmured, a sound that carried more longing than she intended.

Noticing the shift in her tone, Jasper stood quickly, busying himself at the table. "What would you like?" he asked, his voice steady, though his hands fumbled slightly.

Temilola walked toward him, the sheet slipping away, leaving her bare. Jasper froze, his breath hitching, before she darted into the bathroom, self-conscious. Left holding an empty plate, he exhaled sharply, running a hand through his hair.

When she emerged, now wrapped in a towel, Jasper handed her a boutique bag. "I picked this up for you earlier."

Curious, she peeked inside. The vibrant yellow sundress hugged her curves perfectly, and as she slipped it on, Jasper muttered under his breath, "Damn."

Temilola laughed, the tension breaking for a moment. But as Jasper prepared to leave, folding her clothes neatly and placing them on the bed, a heaviness settled between them.

"I'll call you later?" he asked, pausing at the door.

She nodded, her mouth full of food, and he left with a satisfied smile.

As the door clicked shut, reality crashed back in. "Shit, what time is it?" Temilola scrambled for her phone, dread pooling in her stomach. Monday had arrived, and with it, the consequences of stolen moments.

Rebeccah Worship

Chapter 17: Lines Blurred

Remembering Jasmine, Priscilla, and Afryea back home, Temilola carefully packed as much food as she could before heading out. By the time she arrived home, it was just after 7 a.m. The kitchen was quiet, with Jasmine and Priscilla seated at the center island, sipping their coffee.

Temilola walked in, placing the bag of food on the table.

"Takeaway? Where did you go?" Priscilla asked, her tone a mix of shock and curiosity. Her sharp eyes followed her mother's every move as Temilola unpacked the spread.

Priscilla quickly stood and approached, her fingers already reaching for a bagel.

"Grab two plates from the cabinet. Jasmine might want some too," Temilola said, deliberately avoiding Jasmine's gaze.

Dreading the inevitable interrogation about why she hadn't come home the previous night, Temilola busied herself pouring coffee before taking a seat at the island. She hoped the food would serve as a sufficient distraction.

Jasmine, sensing her best friend's unease, broke the silence. "Relax. I think we're just glad you're okay, more than anything else." Her tone was soothing, her words deliberate. "You don't have to tell us anything if you don't want to."

Priscilla, however, wasn't as forgiving. "The hell she doesn't!" she snapped, her frustration cutting through the calm like a blade.

"If I pulled the same stunt, the world would never hear the end of it!" she added, glaring at her mother. "How is it that Ms. Adeniyi goes on a first date with a 20-year-old she should be setting an example for—and then doesn't come home?"

"Whoa, take it easy," Jasmine interjected, her tone firm but placating. "I'm sure Mom had a good reason for not coming home last night. And it might not even be what you think."

Temilola set her coffee cup down firmly, her tone calm but commanding. "Priscilla, I raised you better than this. I will not sit here and listen to you disrespect me in front of our guest," she said, locking eyes with her daughter.

Her next words came measured and steady, their weight undeniable. "We both had too much to drink, and it was safer for us to stay at the event until daybreak." The lie slipped out effortlessly, though it left an ache in her chest.

Priscilla's sharp expression faltered, her anger giving way to guilt. "I'm so sorry, Mom. I didn't know," she murmured, her voice softening. "Jasmine and I were worried about you."

"I'm sorry for not calling you both," Temilola replied, standing from the table. "It was irresponsible of me." She turned toward the stairs, eager to escape the conversation and its prying eyes.

Once in her room, Temilola quickly changed out of the yellow dress Jasper had bought her, slipping into her work clothes. Relief flooded her as she realized neither Jasmine nor Priscilla had commented on the outfit. Moments later, she hurried down the stairs and out of the penthouse, successfully dodging further scrutiny.

Arriving at work just in time for the noon board meeting, Temilola exhaled in relief. Missing another meeting with the directors would have been catastrophic—especially considering one of the new directors was Jasper.

Her thoughts drifted to the last board meeting she had missed, when a briefing had introduced the new members of the board. Jasper's name had been on the list, though she hadn't fully processed it at the time. His recent promotion had not only elevated his status but had also allowed him to purchase significant shares in the company, earning him a coveted seat on the board.

Now, as she took her place at the table, her pulse quickened when her gaze met his. The realization hit her like a lightning bolt: technically, she now worked for him.

Rebeccah Worship

Chapter 18: Shifting Boundaries

Temilola's heart thudded in her chest as she adjusted her blazer and smoothed her skirt, forcing a calm exterior. The polished mahogany table in the boardroom reflected her tense expression as she took her seat. Around her, directors shuffled papers and exchanged greetings, oblivious to the storm brewing within her.

Her eyes darted toward Jasper, seated at the far end of the table. He looked completely at ease, a vision of confidence in his tailored navy suit. His demeanor was professional, but the faint curve of his lips hinted at a private joke—

a secret only they shared. She quickly averted her gaze, focusing instead on the presentation folder in front of her.

The meeting began with the chairman's booming voice welcoming everyone and outlining the agenda. As he spoke, Temilola stole a glance at Jasper. He was listening intently, his hands steepled under his chin. Gone was the man who had whispered her name like a prayer just hours ago. Here sat a formidable business magnate, the weight of his position commanding respect.

Yet, the memory of his touch crept into her mind—the way he had held her as if she were the only thing anchoring him to the world. The raw intensity of their connection had been both terrifying and exhilarating, a depth of passion she hadn't known she craved.

"Temilola?" The chairman's voice snapped her back to the present. She blinked, realizing the room had gone silent. Every eye was on her, including Jasper's, though his held a flicker of amusement.

"Yes," she said, clearing her throat and quickly scanning the agenda. "I believe we were discussing the projections for next quarter?"

The chairman nodded, and she dove into her prepared analysis, her voice steady despite the tremor in her hands. As she spoke, she felt Jasper's gaze linger on her, a steady warmth that made her hyper-aware of every word she said. She refused to meet his eyes, determined to maintain her professionalism.

When the meeting finally adjourned, Temilola busied herself gathering her notes, hoping to slip out unnoticed. But as she turned to leave, a hand lightly brushed her arm. She froze, her pulse quickening.

"Ms. Adeniyi," Jasper said, his tone formal, though his eyes held a teasing glint. "A moment of your time?"

She nodded, keeping her expression neutral. Together, they stepped out into the corridor, the din of departing board members fading behind them.

"What is it?" she asked, crossing her arms defensively. She hated how easily he unsettled her, how effortlessly he chipped away at the walls she'd spent years building.

Jasper leaned against the wall, his posture casual but his gaze intense. "You were brilliant in there," he said, his voice low and smooth. "Though I suspect you were avoiding looking at me the entire time."

Temilola's cheeks flushed, but she lifted her chin. "I was focused on the agenda, Mr. Adiyiah."

His lips twitched into a small smile. "Ah, back to formalities, are we?" He stepped closer, his voice dropping to a whisper. "I wonder if that's how you'll address me tonight."

Her breath hitched, and she stepped back, shaking her head. "Jasper, this isn't a game. You're on the board now. I have a career to protect."

His expression softened, the teasing glint replaced by something more earnest. "And you think I'd jeopardize that? Temilola, what happened between us was real. I'm not asking for anything that would compromise your integrity. I just..." He paused, running a hand through his hair. "I just want to be close to you. On your terms."

The vulnerability in his voice disarmed her. For a moment, she allowed herself to meet his gaze fully. There was no mistaking the sincerity in his eyes, nor the depth of his feelings. But the weight of her responsibilities and the complexity of their connection pressed down on her like a leaden cloak.

"I don't know if I can do this," she said, her voice barely above a whisper.

Jasper nodded, his expression understanding but resolute. "Take all the time you need. Just know I'm not going anywhere."

With that, he turned and walked away, leaving Temilola standing in the empty corridor, her emotions a chaotic swirl of desire, fear, and longing. She watched him disappear around the corner, her heart aching with the knowledge that no matter how much she wanted to resist, she was already in too deep.

At home, Temilola sank onto the couch next to Jasmine, who was sipping tea and scrolling on her phone.

"There she is!" Jasmine exclaimed, setting her tea down. "You can't sneak by me like you did this morning. Spill it—what's going on?"

Temilola groaned and leaned her head on Jasmine's shoulder. "You won't let this go, will you?"

"Nope." Jasmine grinned, gently nudging her friend upright. "Priscilla's out for the night, so now's the perfect time to catch me up. What's the deal with you and Jasper?"

Temilola hesitated, then finally blurted, "We had sex."

Jasmine's eyes widened. "And?"

"And it was amazing," Temilola admitted, her cheeks flushing. "But I'm scared, Jazz. I don't know what I'm doing—or what he really wants."

Jasmine tilted her head thoughtfully. "You think he's not serious?"

"No, that's the thing," Temilola said, wringing her hands. "I think he is. And that terrifies me."

Jasmine smirked. "Girl, you're in love."

Temilola froze, her silence confirming Jasmine's suspicion.

"Have you met his family?" Jasmine asked.

"No…" Temilola frowned, realizing how little she knew about that side of his life. "I've never even asked."

"Maybe it's time you did," Jasmine suggested.

Temilola nodded, pulling out her phone to call Jasper. As his deep, familiar voice answered, her nerves eased.

"Temi?" he said softly, the warmth in his tone wrapping around her like a hug.

"Can we talk tonight?" she asked, her voice trembling slightly.

"Of course," he replied, without hesitation.

As she hung up, Jasmine grinned. "Now, that's progress."

Temilola smiled back, hope blooming in her chest. But beneath it, the fear lingered, whispering that their story was just beginning—and that the next chapter would change everything.

Chapter 19: Navigating New Beginnings

At exactly 9 p.m., the doorbell rang, sending a ripple of nervous energy through Temilola. She hurried to answer it, smoothing invisible creases from her dress. For the last hour, she had been pacing the living room, fluffing pillows, and rearranging the coffee table repeatedly, her nervous energy betraying her calm exterior. Jasmine, sensing the tension, had retreated upstairs earlier with a smirk and a cheerful, "Good luck!"

When Temilola opened the door, Jasper stood there, a bottle of wine in each hand and a boyish grin lighting up his face. His casual yet polished outfit—a crisp white shirt with the sleeves rolled up and tailored slacks—highlighted his effortless charm.

"Good evening, Temi," he greeted, the nickname rolling off his tongue as if it had always belonged to her.

"Good evening," she replied, stepping aside to let him in. She tried to keep her composure, but the warmth in his gaze made her pulse quicken.

Jasper handed her the wine and looked around the living room, taking in its cozy atmosphere. "Your home suits you—warm and inviting."

"Thank you," she said, gesturing for him to sit. She disappeared into the kitchen to fetch two glasses, taking the moment to steady her breathing.

When she returned, she found Jasper standing by the bookshelf, holding a framed photo of Priscilla and Afryea as children.

"She's grown into a remarkable woman," he remarked, pointing to Priscilla. "You've done a great job raising her."

Temilola smiled softly, the compliment warming her. "Thank you. It hasn't been easy, but she's my world."

Jasper turned to her, his expression shifting to one of earnest admiration. "And yet, you still manage to be an incredible professional, a supportive mother, and somehow the most captivating woman I've ever met."

Her breath caught at the intensity of his words, leaving her momentarily speechless. To break the tension, she poured the wine and handed him a glass.

"Let's sit," she said, motioning toward the couch.

The initial conversation was light, filled with banter about work, favorite wines, and shared laughs over memories from the boardroom. But as the night deepened, their dialogue grew more personal.

"Jasper," Temilola began hesitantly, "I've realized something. We've spent so much time together, yet I know so little about your family. I've never asked about your parents or—"

He raised a hand, stopping her mid-sentence, his expression heavy. "It's okay, Temi. You don't have to tiptoe around it."

Setting his glass down, he leaned back, running a hand through his hair. "My parents passed away when I was in my early twenties. It was sudden—a car accident. Afryea was still a teenager. Losing them was... devastating."

Temilola placed a comforting hand on his arm. "I'm so sorry. I can't imagine how hard that must have been."

He nodded, his gaze distant. "It was. But it forced me to grow up fast. I became Afryea's guardian, took over my father's marketing firm, and poured everything into building a life where she'd never have to worry. She's my anchor, my motivation for everything."

Temilola's admiration for him deepened. "You've done an amazing job. Afryea is a remarkable young woman—strong, compassionate, and ambitious. That's a reflection of you."

Jasper's eyes softened as they met hers. "Hearing that from you means more than you know."

They sat in silence, the weight of his confession lingering. Then he reached for her hand, his thumb brushing against her knuckles.

"Temi, I didn't plan for this—for us. But meeting you has been... transformative. You make me want to be better, to risk everything for something real."

Her heart swelled, yet fear tempered her joy. "Jasper, I feel the same way. But this... whatever this is, it's complicated. Our careers, our families—it's a lot."

"I know," he said softly. "And I'm not asking for answers tonight. I just want you to trust me. Trust that I'm here for the long haul."

His sincerity shone through, and slowly, she nodded. "Alright, Jasper. Let's take it one step at a time."

He smiled, raising his glass in a silent toast. She clinked hers against his, allowing herself a fragile hope for the future.

When Jasper left, the house felt too quiet. Leaning against the door, Temilola replayed the night in her mind, her heart full yet weighed down by the complexities ahead. Upstairs, Jasmine's light glowed faintly under her door, but Temilola decided to leave the questions for the morning. Tonight, she needed time to reflect.

The next morning, the smell of fresh coffee lured Temilola to the kitchen. Jasmine was at the stove, humming as she stirred something.

"Morning, lover girl," Jasmine teased, glancing over her shoulder.

Temilola chuckled, pouring herself a mug of coffee. "It wasn't a rendezvous. We just talked."

Jasmine smirked. "Uh-huh. And?"

"He opened up about his parents and raising Afryea. It was... eye-opening."

Jasmine's expression softened. "He sounds like more than just a charmer. That's good. You deserve someone solid."

Temilola nodded, her thoughts circling back to Jasper's words. Maybe it was time to take a leap of faith—not just for Jasper, but for herself.

Rebeccah Worship

Chapter 20: Under the Jasmine Moon

The next morning, the doorbell rang just as Priscilla descended the stairs in her pajamas. She opened the door to find a delivery man holding an elegant box wrapped in gold paper.

"Delivery for Ms. Adeniyi," he announced with a professional smile.

Priscilla furrowed her brows, accepting the package and signing for it before closing the door. The box felt surprisingly heavy. Her curiosity grew as she noticed an embossed logo on the packaging. Carrying it into the kitchen, she set it on the counter and called out, "Mom! You've got a delivery!"

Temilola appeared moments later, coffee mug in hand. "A delivery? Who's it from?"

Priscilla handed her the attached card. Temilola opened it, her breath hitching as she read the note inside:

Temi,
I couldn't stop thinking about you. I hope this small gift brings a smile to your face. I'd love the honor of joining you for dinner soon—perhaps Saturday? I'll bring the wine.
Yours,
Jasper

Her fingers trembled slightly as she began unwrapping the box. Priscilla, brimming with curiosity, leaned in.

When the wrapping paper came off, Temilola gasped. Inside was a stunning beige Lana Marks clutch with 18-karat gold trimming. The calf leather gleamed, a testament to its flawless craftsmanship.

Priscilla's eyes widened. "Mom… is that what I think it is? That purse costs, like, twenty grand!"

Temilola shook her head, stunned. "Jasper sent me this?"

Priscilla smirked. "I mean, he *did* call you 'forever mine' on the phone. Looks like he's putting his money where his mouth is."

"Priscilla!" Temilola admonished, giving her a sharp look. "It's not about the money— it's just… extravagant. And what will people think?"

Priscilla shrugged. "That Jasper Adiyiah has good taste? Relax, Mom. If it makes you uncomfortable, just tell him."

Temilola carefully closed the box, her emotions swirling. Part of her felt flattered and thrilled by Jasper's gesture, but another part couldn't help but feel apprehensive. This wasn't just flirtation—this was something more. And that scared her.

The aroma of jollof rice, fried plantains, and peppered goat soup wafted through the house as Temilola added finishing touches to the table. Priscilla had helped her prepare the meal but had spent most of the time teasing her about her "dinner date."

When the doorbell rang, Temilola's heart skipped a beat. She opened the door to find Jasper standing there with his trademark confidence, holding two bottles of sweet red wine. He wore a crisp white shirt, its sleeves rolled up to reveal strong forearms and tailored dark slacks.

"You look stunning," Jasper said, his voice low as he handed her the wine. His eyes lingered on her for a moment before glancing at the table behind her. "And dinner smells amazing."

Temilola smiled, ushering him in. During dinner, the conversation flowed effortlessly, punctuated by laughter. Jasper's charm seemed effortless, and even Priscilla, who joined them, found herself warming to him.

After dessert, Temilola leaned forward, her tone measured. "Jasper, there's something I'd like to discuss."

He set his wine glass down, giving her his full attention. "I'm listening."

"It's about Afryea," Temilola began, her voice tentative. "I know she means the world to you, and I don't want to overstep, but... I was thinking it might be easier for you to focus on work if she came to live with me and Priscilla."

Jasper's brow furrowed in surprise but softened as he listened. Temilola hurried to clarify.

"I don't want to disrupt the bond you two share. I just thought... maybe it would ease the burden a bit. She's practically family to us, and we'd love to have her. But only if you think it's a good idea."

Jasper leaned back, his gaze thoughtful. "That's incredibly generous, Temi. You're right—it would make things easier for me. But I'm not sure how Afryea would feel. She's fiercely independent and might see it as me pushing her away."

Temilola nodded, understanding. "Of course. I don't want her to feel cast aside. It's just an option I wanted to put out there."

Jasper reached across the table, placing his hand gently over hers. "Thank you for thinking of her. I'll talk to Afryea. I trust her to decide what's best."

The conversation shifted to lighter topics, but Temilola couldn't help the warmth that spread through her chest. Jasper's attentiveness and willingness to listen deepened feelings she hadn't wanted to name—feelings that thrilled and terrified her in equal measure.

After dinner, Temilola suggested they take a walk in the park near her penthouse. Jasper readily agreed. Priscilla cleared the dishes and excused herself to bed, leaving the two alone.

The park was a serene oasis in bustling Ikoyi, with well-lit paths winding through lush greenery. The soft glow of streetlamps cast a golden hue on the foliage, and the gentle breeze carried the faint scent of roses, hibiscus, and blooming jasmine.

Temilola hesitated when they reached a shaded trail near the pond. The dense canopy overhead allowed only faint moonlight to filter through, giving the path a secluded, almost enchanted feel.

"I'm not sure about this," she murmured.

Jasper squeezed her hand. "Trust me, Temi. I'm here. You're safe."

Taking a deep breath, she allowed him to lead her into the dim trail. The world grew quieter with each step, the pond beside them shimmering under the moonlight.

At a bend in the path, Jasper stopped abruptly. Turning to face her, he gently cupped her face. "Temi," he whispered, his voice thick with emotion.

Before she could respond, his lips met hers. The kiss was tender yet electric, a surge of unspoken desire and affection. Her breath caught as she melted into him, her hands finding his chest.

His arms wrapped around her, pulling her closer, as if trying to erase the space between them. Time seemed to stop as their passion took over. The soft grass and fallen leaves beneath their feet cushioned them as they lowered to the ground, their hands exploring, their breaths mingling.

The air around them seemed to hum with energy, the secluded trail becoming their private sanctuary. The moonlight cast a silvery glow on their skin, and the rustling trees above provided a natural rhythm to their movements.

Their connection grew deeper with every touch, every whispered word of affection. It wasn't just passion—it was a moment of emotional vulnerability, a bond that felt unshakable. Afterward, they lay together on the soft earth, the world around them still and peaceful. Jasper gently brushed a strand of hair from Temilola's face, his eyes filled with an adoration that made her chest tighten.

She smiled, tracing small circles on his chest, neither of them speaking, content in the quiet intimacy they had shared. Eventually, they redressed, taking their time to straighten their clothes and compose themselves.

Jasper helped Temilola to her feet, his hand lingering in hers as if reluctant to let go. As they made their way back to the penthouse, the atmosphere between them felt different— richer, more profound.

The connection they had forged under the quiet canopy of the trail seemed to linger in the air, a bond neither could ignore. When they arrived at the penthouse, they exchanged a lingering goodnight at the door.

Temilola smiled softly as she watched Jasper walk away, her heart full and her mind buzzing with the memory of their time together.

Chapter 21: Crossroads Over Dinner

The following morning, just as Afryea was rushing out the door to Priscilla's place, Jasper stopped her. Standing by the doorway with a serious expression, he was clearly ready for a conversation.

"It's about what Temilola suggested," Jasper began.

Afryea frowned, confusion mixed with irritation. "Bro, I don't get it. How long have you two even been dating? What, you guys just sit there gossiping about me now?"

Her tone was sharp, but her expression betrayed hurt. Tears threatened to spill as she continued, "Listen, I've been friends with Priscilla for years, and I've never suggested anything like that to her or her mom. If you don't want me here anymore, just say it. I can move back to Mom and Dad's house. The housekeepers still live there, so I won't even be alone."

Jasper stepped forward, softening his tone as he pulled her into a comforting embrace. "You know that's not what I mean," he said gently, holding her for a moment before pulling back to meet her eyes.

"I think Temilola only suggested it because you and Priscilla grew up like sisters. She doesn't want you to feel neglected. Or maybe Priscilla put her up to it when she found out."

"Found out about what?" Afryea asked, wiping her eyes.

Jasper sighed, sadness creeping into his voice. "I told Temilola about Mom and Dad's car accident on our last date."

Afryea's anger softened as the weight of his words sank in. "I told Priscilla the second I found out. We've been inseparable ever since."

Jasper frowned. "So Priscilla never told her mom?"

Afryea shook her head. "Her mom used to travel a lot for work. That might be why."

Jasper nodded slowly, considering this. "Hmm... so, what should I tell Temilola?"

Afryea hesitated. "Can I think about it?"

"Of course," Jasper said with a small smile. "Just let me know as soon as you can. I'd like to have an answer for her by our next date."

"Thanks, bro." Afryea gave him a quick hug before rushing out the door.

When Afryea arrived at Priscilla's penthouse, she stormed into the kitchen, dropping her backpack onto the center island with a loud thud. Crossing her arms, she glared at Priscilla, frustration radiating off her.

"Uh-oh," Priscilla said, rolling her eyes. "What did I do this time?"

Before Afryea could respond, Temilola entered the kitchen, mug in hand.

"Morning, ladies!" she chirped, taking a sip of her coffee before heading out the door.

Once the door clicked shut, Priscilla turned to Afryea. "Okay, spill it. What's the problem? What did I do?"

"It's not you," Afryea said, her voice tense. "It's your mom."

"My mom? What about her?"

"She told my brother to kick me out so I could move in here with you," Afryea replied, her voice dripping with sarcasm.

Priscilla stared at her before bursting into laughter. "Kick you out? Afryea, come on. You're overreacting."

"I'm not overreacting," Afryea snapped.

Priscilla smirked. "Sis, you know your brother's too busy to take care of you, and honestly, my mom's the same way. But I'm here for you, and you know it. Why not just move in already?"

Afryea hesitated, her defensiveness cracking. "You really think I'd be better off living with you?"

Priscilla shrugged. "Of course. You'd have more freedom here, and we could actually spend time together. Plus, you wouldn't be imposing. If anything, you'd be doing me a favor."

Afryea raised an eyebrow. "A favor?"

"Yeah. It gets lonely sometimes. And we could finally do those crazy theme nights we're always talking about."

A small laugh escaped Afryea. "You mean the ones where you insist on karaoke and I end up doing all the singing?"

"Exactly," Priscilla grinned, throwing an arm around her.

"Alright," Afryea said with a faint smile. "I'll think about it."

"Think about it, or say yes?"

Afryea rolled her eyes. "I'll give you an answer soon."

"Deal," Priscilla said, holding out her pinky.

With a sigh, Afryea linked her pinky with Priscilla's.

That evening, Afryea and Priscilla arrived at an elegant restaurant where Temilola had reserved a table. The warm lighting and soft jazz music created a relaxed atmosphere.

"Evening, ladies," Temilola greeted them as they approached.

After quick pleasantries, Temilola got to the point. "I wanted to talk about... some changes that might help everyone feel more supported."

"Mom," Priscilla interjected, "just say it. You want Afryea to move in with me."

Temilola smiled slightly. "Yes. I think it would be good for both of you. You're practically sisters already."

Afryea opened her mouth to protest, but Priscilla cut her off. "Mom, we've got this. If Afryea wants to move in, she will. Right, Afryea?"

All eyes turned to her. Taking a deep breath, Afryea found her voice. "I appreciate the thought, aunty. But I need to decide for myself."

Temilola nodded, her expression soft. "Of course. Take your time."

As the night continued, the conversation lightened, but Afryea couldn't shake the feeling that she stood at a crossroads. Whatever choice she made, life was about to change.

Rebeccah Worship

Chapter 22: Breaking Barriers

Jasper inherited his father's marketing firm after his passing, a transition that might have been chaotic if not for an unexpected twist. A year before his death, Jasper's father had unknowingly set him up to intern at the firm— a decision that proved invaluable. By the time Jasper assumed the role of president, he already knew the business inside and out, easing the burden of stepping into his father's shoes.

When Jasper wasn't immersed in the firm or pursuing other ventures, his mind was consumed by thoughts of Temilola. He had fallen deeply in love with her, but her recent suggestion—that Afryea should stay with her and Priscilla so she wouldn't feel neglected— left him conflicted. He suspected the gesture stemmed from guilt over not knowing about his parents' passing, despite Afryea and Priscilla being best friends.

"I hate all this tiptoeing around," Jasper muttered, frustration simmering beneath the surface. "I want to wake up next to Temilola, not come home to an empty house."

Determined to deepen their relationship, he made a decision. "God help me—it took me two months just to get a kiss," he thought, a wry smile tugging at his lips.

With newfound resolve, Jasper left work early, stopping by a store to gather ingredients for dinner and a small gift for Temilola. Once home, he called her, his deep voice radiating warmth through the line.

"Hi, beautiful," he greeted.

Temilola's giggle betrayed her delight. "Hi, yourself."

"I know we just had dinner a few days ago, but I can't stop thinking about you. Can we have dinner tonight?" he asked, his tone tinged with hope.

"Sure," she replied. "At my place, or are you picking me up?"

"I'll pick you up at 7 p.m.," he said, a grin spreading across his face, though she couldn't see it.

Before leaving, Jasper prepared the meal and borrowed his late father's sleek black Rolls-Royce Cullinan. Arriving at Temilola's penthouse precisely at 7 p.m., he found her descending the staircase in a stunning, curve-hugging red dress paired with gold and diamond accessories. She carried the Lana Marks clutch he had gifted her the week before.

"You look breathtaking," he said, his voice low and reverent as he met her at the bottom of the steps. Pulling her in for a kiss, he lingered for just a moment before leading her out.

As they approached the car, Temilola's eyes widened. "You own a Rolls-Royce?" she asked, trying to sound nonchalant.

"It's a Cullinan," Jasper clarified. "And no, it was my father's."

Not wanting to press further, she shifted the conversation. "So, where are we going?"

"My place," Jasper replied with a warm smile.

Temilola was awestruck upon entering his home. From the carefully curated paintings to the sculptures adorning the space, the house exuded elegance. "Your place is beautiful," she said, her voice tinged with admiration.

"Thank you," Jasper said. "My mom decorated everything here."

Temilola's expression softened. "I wish I'd taken the time to get to know your parents," she said, her voice wavering with guilt.

Jasper stepped closer, wrapping his arms around her. "Don't feel bad. My parents knew all about you. They wouldn't let their only daughter spend days with a stranger," he teased, trying to lighten the mood.

"They knew me?" Temilola asked, wide-eyed.

Jasper nodded, recounting how his mother had once personally taken a sick Afryea to school so she wouldn't miss Priscilla's birthday.

Relief flooded her face, and they both laughed, the tension easing.

Over dinner, Jasper unveiled his mother's signature Jollof spaghetti recipe.

"Your mom taught you how to cook?" Temilola asked, visibly impressed.

"She taught me everything," Jasper replied fondly.

The evening unfolded with laughter, wine, and even an impromptu dance in the living room. As the night wound down, Jasper retrieved a small black box.

"Relax, it's not what you think," he teased when he saw Temilola's eyes widen.

Inside was a slip of paper with five numbers.

"What is this?" she asked, confused.

"It's the code to my house," Jasper explained with a tender smile. "Besides Afryea, you're the only person who has it."

Temilola stared at him, overwhelmed. "You're giving me access to your home? This is serious, Jasper."

"Yes, it is," he replied earnestly.

Overcome, Temilola leaned in, her lips meeting his in a kiss that conveyed gratitude and a love that words couldn't capture.

"Temi," Jasper whispered against her lips, his voice heavy with emotion, "you mean everything to me."

Temilola pulled back slightly, her eyes searching his. "This is a big step, Jasper. Are you sure?"

He nodded without hesitation. "I've never been more sure. I want you in my life—fully."

Tears shimmered in her eyes as she smiled. "You have no idea how much that means to me."

As the night deepened, they settled on the plush sofa in the living room. Jasper poured more wine, their fingers intertwined as they discussed lighter topics.

"About what I said the other day—Afryea staying with me and Priscilla," Temilola began hesitantly. "I didn't mean to overstep. I just want to help."

Jasper sighed, running a hand through his hair. "I've thought about it. I know you care about her, and I think she'd love being with you. But I don't want her to feel like I'm passing her off."

Temilola nodded. "I'd never want her to feel that way either. I just admire everything you've done for her and want to support you."

Jasper smiled, squeezing her hand. "Thank you. I'll talk to her. If she's open to it, we'll make it work."

The conversation circled back to laughter and shared dreams as the bond between them solidified. By the time Jasper walked Temilola to the door, their connection felt unshakable.

Chapter 23: Foundations of A Family

The next afternoon, Jasper had lunch with his sister, Afryea. His face lit up with a constant smile, and Afryea couldn't help but notice his buoyant mood. It was obvious to her that his good spirits had little to do with their meal or work.

"You're really into her, huh?" Afryea teased, her voice dripping with playful sarcasm as she speared a piece of fried plantain with her fork.

"You have no idea," Jasper replied, chuckling as he took a sip of his drink.

Later that evening, at a cozy Lagos restaurant filled with the faint hum of conversation and soft Wizkid tunes playing in the background, Jasper and Afryea savored plates of jollof spaghetti with fried chicken and plantains. It was here that Jasper decided to broach a topic he'd been mulling over since the previous night.

"Afryea," he began cautiously, setting down his fork. "I've been thinking… I want us to move back home, and I'd like your thoughts."

Afryea raised an eyebrow, leaning back in her seat. "Back to Mom and Dad's house? Seriously?"

"Yes," Jasper said, pausing before adding, "and that's not all."

Afryea's curiosity deepened. "What else?"

"I want Temilola and Priscilla to move in with us," Jasper said firmly, meeting her gaze.

For a moment, Afryea stared at him, her face blank as she processed his words. Then, she burst into uncontrollable laughter, her head thrown back, drawing stares from nearby tables.

"Afryea!" Jasper hissed, his face reddening. "What's wrong with you? Get a hold of yourself."

Struggling to compose herself, Afryea wiped her eyes and leaned forward, her tone incredulous. "You're joking, right? Do you think Temilola is some teenager fresh out of high school? That woman raised a child and built an empire in under ten years!"

Her words were sharp, and her animated gestures drew even more attention. Jasper sighed, dropping his fork onto his plate.

Noticing his deflated posture, Afryea softened. "Look, I get it," she said gently, resuming her meal. "Moving back won't bring them back, you know?"

Jasper's voice dropped to a wistful tone. "But it could make us a family again."

Afryea froze mid-bite, raising a skeptical brow. "Wait—which family? Who's the wife?"

Jasper chuckled. "Temilola, of course."

Afryea nearly choked on her laughter. "Five months of dating, and you're already calling her your wife?"

They laughed together, the tension lifting as they shifted to lighter topics. As they headed home, Afryea asked Jasper to drop her off at Priscilla's house.

As they pulled into the driveway, Jasper turned to her with a serious look. "Can you keep our earlier conversation between us for now?"

Feigning innocence, Afryea grinned mischievously. "What conversation?"

Jasper sighed. "The one about moving back to Mom and Dad's house."

"Oh, that? Sure. Forgotten already," she teased, stepping out of the car with a sly smile.

The next morning, Jasper awoke with a sense of clarity. He'd spent the night mulling over his conversation with Afryea and Temilola's earlier suggestion about Afryea moving in with her and Priscilla. It wasn't a bad idea, but it raised deeper questions about the life he wanted to build.

By mid-afternoon, Jasper found himself parked outside Temilola's penthouse. He'd texted earlier, asking to drop by, and she'd quickly agreed.

Now, stepping into her elegantly styled home, he was struck again by how perfectly it reflected her—sophisticated, warm, and undeniably captivating.

Temilola stood in the kitchen, her gold bracelets jingling softly as she prepared lunch. Jasper leaned against the doorframe, watching her with an affectionate smile.

"You're gaping again," she said without looking up, her lips curving into a playful smirk.

"Can you blame me?" he replied, stepping closer.

She laughed, shaking her head. "What's on your mind, Jasper?"

He hesitated, his smile fading. "I need to talk to you about something important."

Temilola turned to face him, her expression curious. "Alright. What is it?"

Jasper took a deep breath. "You know how you suggested Afryea move in with you and Priscilla?"

She nodded, cautious.

"Well," he continued, "I've been thinking. I think we should all move in together—but not at your place. At my parents' house."

Temilola tilted her head, surprised but intrigued. "The house you grew up in?"

Jasper nodded. "It's big enough for all of us, and it's full of memories. I think it could be the foundation for something amazing. A real family. You, me, Priscilla, and Afryea."

Temilola stared at him, her expression unreadable. Then she walked to the living room, motioning for him to follow. Once seated, she met his gaze.

"Jasper, that's... a lot," she said. "I understand why it's important to you. And I love that you're thinking about the future. But I've spent my whole life being independent. Even with you giving me the key to your house, I'm still adjusting to letting someone in."

"I know," Jasper said gently, taking her hand. "But I don't want to keep living separately. I want us to be a family. Priscilla deserves to grow up surrounded by love. And Afryea... she needs you, too."

Temilola's eyes softened as she glanced down at their entwined hands. "You're serious about this, aren't you?"

"I am," Jasper said. "But I don't want to pressure you. This is a big step, and I want it to feel right."

After a moment, Temilola smiled, tentative but genuine. "Let me think about it," she said softly.

Jasper brushed a kiss against her forehead. "Take all the time you need."

As sunlight streamed through the windows, Jasper felt a flicker of hope. This wasn't just a step toward building a life together; it was the foundation of something lasting and beautiful. Something worth fighting for.

Chapter 24: Unspoken Bonds

As the afternoon softened into evening, Priscilla bounded into the living room, her notebook clutched in one hand and a pencil in the other. Her excitement was infectious, drawing a smile from Jasper even before she spoke.

"Uncle Jasper!" she called, settling herself on the armrest of his chair. "Are you staying for movie night? Mom said I get to pick the movie!"

Jasper chuckled, pulling her into a quick side hug. "Already calling the shots, huh?"

Priscilla grinned mischievously. "Always. So, are you staying?"

Before he could respond, Temilola appeared in the doorway, carrying a small bowl of popcorn. She raised an eyebrow at Priscilla's enthusiasm. "What's this about movie night?"

"Priscilla's campaigning for my attendance," Jasper said, his tone light.

Temilola sat on the couch, setting the popcorn on the table. "She's very persuasive. You don't stand a chance."

Priscilla, ever the actress, gave Jasper her most imploring puppy-dog eyes.

He laughed, throwing up his hands in surrender. "Alright, you win. I'm staying."

Priscilla cheered, bolting off to fetch the list of movies she'd meticulously curated.

Not long after, Afryea joined them, settling beside Temilola and eyeing the growing snack pile. "I hope you picked a good one, Priscilla," she teased.

Priscilla returned, holding her notebook aloft like a trophy. "We're watching *The Lion King*! Uncle Jasper, you'll love it!"

Jasper leaned back, laughing. "An excellent choice, kiddo. A true classic."

The movie night unfolded with laughter echoing through the room. Priscilla recited her favorite lines with theatrical flair, drawing giggles from everyone. Temilola relaxed against the couch armrest, her hand occasionally brushing Jasper's as they reached for snacks simultaneously.

For a fleeting moment, Jasper let himself revel in the scene—a snapshot of the life he wanted to build.

By the time the movie ended, Priscilla had fallen asleep, her head resting on Afryea's lap. As Temilola gathered the empty bowls, Jasper joined her in the kitchen.

"Nights like this," he began, leaning against the counter, "make me sure about what I want."

Temilola paused, looking at him curiously. "And what's that?"

Jasper's gaze softened. "This. Us. A family. It feels right, doesn't it?"

Temilola smiled, but a flicker of uncertainty danced in her eyes.

When it was time for Jasper to leave, Temilola walked him to the door.

"Thanks for staying," she said softly.

"Thanks for having me." Jasper leaned in, brushing a kiss against her cheek. "Goodnight, Temi."

"Goodnight, Jasper," she replied, watching him step into the elevator before closing the door.

Leaning against it for a moment, she sighed, her mind racing. Glancing toward the living room where Afryea was tucking a blanket around Priscilla, she picked up her phone and dialed Jasmine.

"Hey," she said when her best friend answered. "Are you free to talk?"

Jasmine's warm, teasing voice came through. "Depends. Is this about a certain someone who drives a Cullinan and has you glowing lately?"

Temilola sighed, though a small smile tugged at her lips. "It's more serious than that, Jas. I need your advice."

"Alright," Jasmine said, her tone shifting to concern. "Tell me everything."

The next morning, sunlight spilled into the kitchen, illuminating the marble countertops. Priscilla sat at the breakfast table, stirring her cereal distractedly. Her tablet sat propped up, forgotten. Across the room, Afryea leaned against the counter, cradling her tea.

"Morning," Afryea said, her voice uncharacteristically hesitant.

Priscilla looked up, frowning slightly. "Morning. You okay? You look...off."

Afryea sighed, setting her mug down. "There's something I need to tell you, and you might not like it."

Priscilla straightened, her curiosity piqued. "What's going on?"

Afryea joined her at the table, clasping her hands tightly. "It's about Jasper. He suggested something last night, and I thought you should hear it from me first."

Priscilla's brows knitted. "What did he say?"

Taking a breath, Afryea said, "He thinks we should all move back to his parents' house. He believes it's a way to bring us all together—him, your mom, you, and me."

Priscilla's face froze, her eyes wide. "What?"

"I know it's not what we planned," Afryea said gently. "But Jasper thinks—"

"He thinks?" Priscilla interrupted, her voice rising. "We were supposed to move into the penthouse! This was our plan, Afryea, not his!"

Afryea reached for her hand, but Priscilla pulled away, anger flashing in her eyes. "A fresh start? For who? This was supposed to be *our* home!"

"Priscilla, I get it. I do," Afryea said, her voice steady. "But Jasper's intentions are good. He wants—"

"He wants *everything* to be about him!" Priscilla snapped, standing abruptly.

Afryea rose too, her expression pained. "I know you're upset, and I don't blame you. But no matter what happens, we'll figure it out together."

Priscilla turned away, her voice trembling. "It's not fair, Afryea. This was our chance for something new. Now it feels like I don't even have a say in my own life."

Afryea stepped closer, placing a tentative hand on her shoulder. "You'll always have me, no matter where we are. That won't change."

Priscilla shrugged off her hand, tears slipping down her cheeks. "It already feels like it's changing."

The kitchen fell into heavy silence as the weight of uncertainty pressed down on them both. Though they sat together, the unspoken tension between them left them feeling worlds apart.

Chapter 25: Shifting Sands

When Afryea returned home that evening, her thoughts were heavy with the fallout from her earlier conversation with Priscilla. She walked past Jasper, who was seated at the dining table eating a sandwich, without acknowledging him—a rare occurrence. Jasper noticed instantly but said nothing, letting her retreat into her room.

Afryea tossed her backpack onto the floor and stood motionless, caught between a desire to cry and an urge to shut the world out. She finally sank onto her bed, staring at the ceiling, willing the tension to dissipate.

Moments later, Jasper appeared, swinging her door open with an exaggerated flair. "Kramer from *Seinfeld*, making an entrance!" he declared, grinning.

Afryea flinched, startled. "Jasper! What are you doing? Oh my God, get out!" she exclaimed as he flopped onto her bed on top of her.

"Not until you tell me why you're ignoring me," Jasper replied with a mischievous smile.

Afryea groaned, squirming under his weight. "Fine! Just get off me—you're too heavy!"

Jasper laughed but obliged, rolling onto his side. "You've been acting weird since you got home. Spill."

Afryea sighed, sitting up and running a hand through her curls. "I've got a lot on my mind."

"Does this have anything to do with what you told Priscilla?" Jasper asked, his voice taking on a serious note.

Afryea winced. "Maybe…"

Jasper's eyes narrowed. "I told you not to say anything, Afryea."

"I know! I'm sorry," she said, guilt written across her face. "But she kept asking questions, and I couldn't lie. Now she's upset and thinks you're trying to mess up her mom's life."

Jasper leaned back, frowning. "What exactly did she say?"

Afryea hesitated before answering. "She feels like you're forcing everyone into your idea of a family and taking away her home. She's scared, Jasper."

Jasper sighed, rubbing the bridge of his nose. "I get that this is hard for her. But I'm not trying to take anything away. I'm trying to build something better—for all of us."

"But moving to the mansion will change everything," Afryea said softly. "Priscilla loves the penthouse. And I've lived here with you for five years—it's been home since Mom and Dad died. If we move, I'll barely see her."

Jasper considered her words for a moment, then said, "If we all lived at the mansion, you wouldn't lose that connection. It's bigger, but it could feel like home too."

Afryea shook her head. "It's not that simple, Jasper. Home isn't just a place—it's what we've built here. Priscilla feels like you're asking her to give that up without a say."

The room fell silent. Jasper finally stood, his expression a mix of frustration and understanding. "We'll figure this out," he said, his tone softer.

The next morning, Jasper was dressed for work when he found Afryea slipping on her sneakers by the door.

"Hey," he said, catching her attention. "About last night—I get it. Change is hard, especially for Priscilla. I'll talk to her and try to ease her worries. But she'll always have a place in the house where her mom is."

Afryea nodded, relieved. "Thanks, Jasper. That means a lot."

As he reached for his briefcase, Jasper hesitated. "By the way, did you tell Priscilla about the Davido tickets?"

Afryea froze, her face betraying her guilt. "That… was months ago. I can't remember."

Jasper groaned, rolling his eyes. "Unbelievable. Now I have to go buy VIP tickets to make up for it."

Afryea grinned sheepishly. "Oops?"

Shaking his head, Jasper opened the door. "Let's go before I change my mind about dropping you off."

Afryea grabbed her backpack and followed him out, her spirits lighter despite the uncertainty ahead.

Rebeccah Worship

Chapter 26: Unexpected Proposals

Later that evening, Jasper called Afryea while she was still at Priscilla's house. After many rings, she finally answered, her tone casual.

"Hey," she greeted, knowing it was her brother.

"What the hell took you so long?" Jasper snapped, irritation lacing his voice. "I bet if it were one of those ugly guys you and Priscilla call friends, you'd have rushed to answer."

Afryea rolled her eyes, holding back a laugh. "Who calls someone just to yell at them?

Relax, Jasper. I was in the kitchen—it took me a minute to get to my phone." She glanced at Priscilla, making exaggerated faces to convey her brother's mood.

"Fine, whatever," Jasper grumbled. "Are you free? Can you talk for a few minutes?"

"Yeah, I'm free. It's just me and Priscilla here," she replied, leaning back on the couch.

"Good," Jasper said, his tone softening. "Look, Afryea, if Mom or Dad were still here, I'd be talking to them about this. But they're not, and you're the only person I can trust with this. I need you on my team."

"I'm always on your team," Afryea assured him, a hint of confusion in her voice. "What's going on?"

Noticing her sudden change in demeanor, Priscilla mouthed, *"Everything okay?"* Afryea nodded subtly, signaling all was fine—for now.

"Yesterday, it felt like you were more on Priscilla's side than mine," Jasper continued. "But I'm not here to argue. I've been thinking about our conversation, and I think I've found a solution."

Afryea raised an eyebrow, skeptical. "Hold on. The last time you said you had a solution to anything involving Temilola, it didn't exactly go as planned. What now?"

"See? This is why I don't tell you anything—you're always so negative," Jasper shot back, his frustration bubbling up.

"Alright, alright, I'm sorry," Afryea said, holding up a hand as if he could see her. "It's just that I just smoothed things over with potential VIP Davido tickets, and I'd rather not deal with another storm today."

Ignoring her jab about the tickets, Jasper pressed on. "I've decided to take my relationship with Temilola to the next level."

Afryea sat up straighter, her skepticism giving way to concern. "Okay… and what does that mean?"

"I'm going to propose to her. In a few weeks," Jasper said, his voice steady but firm.

The words hit Afryea like a freight train. She froze, her mouth slightly open, and for a moment, the line was silent.

"Hello? Afryea? Are you still there?" Jasper's voice broke through the quiet, tinged with worry.

"Yes, I'm here," she said finally, though her voice sounded distant, even to herself. "Can we talk about this when I get home? I don't want to discuss it right now." Without waiting for his response, she ended the call abruptly.

Priscilla, who had been watching her friend closely, leaned in. "Whoa! I've never seen that look on your face before. Are you okay? Is Jasper okay? You look like you just saw a ghost!"

Afryea didn't respond immediately. She stared ahead, her mind racing, replaying Jasper's revelation in an endless loop.

"Afryea?" Priscilla nudged her, her concern deepening. "Did you stop breathing or something? What's going on?"

Afryea finally blinked, shaking her head slightly as if snapping out of a trance. "I… I don't know," she whispered.

Priscilla frowned. "Well, whatever it is, I'm here, okay? You don't have to figure it out alone."

But Afryea didn't reply. Her thoughts were elsewhere, tangled in the implications of her brother's decision and what it might mean for all of their lives.

Made in the USA
Columbia, SC
18 March 2025

55303430R00126